These Niggas Ain't Loyal 3

Lock Down Publications
Presents
These Niggas Ain't Loyal 3
A Novel by *Nikki Tee*

Lock Down Publications

P.O. Box 1482
Pine Lake, Ga 30072-1482

Visit our website at www.lockdownpublications.com

First Edition October 2015
Printed in the United States of America

Lock Down Publications
Like our page on Facebook: Lock Down Publications @www.facebook.com/lockdownpublications.ldp
Facebook: Author Nikki Tee
Email: msnikkit504@gmail.com
Cover design and layout by: Dynasty's Cover Me
Book interior design by: Shawn Walker
Edited by: Tumika Cain

DEDICATION

I began writing this series as an outlet to help me cope through the pain and heartbreak of losing one of the most important men in my life. Every day was a struggle. Not being able to wake up to your 5am phone calls devastated me. It was such a huge part of my daily routine. Then one day, that routine changed and the 5am phone calls ceased to exist. I think about you every day. I will never forgot the times we shared and the life lessons you taught me. This book is dedicated to the one man who can never be replaced, my father, Robert Anthony "Beenie" Daliet. I love and miss you, daddy.

ACKNOWLEDGEMENT

Wow! Where to begin? I have to thank my husband Kev for supporting me. It's us against the world. I owe an immense amount of gratitude to my A-1s since Day 1, Quintina Torregano, Robin Torregano, Kendra Torregano, Shwann Torregano, and Trinesha Torregano. You guys have supported me and encouraged me to continue to write this story. When I doubted myself you guys were always there to keep me moving forward. Thank yall for believing in me when I didn't believe in myself. The love you guys have for my story is real. I love you blood sisters.

I have one of the most amazing, positive and encouraging editors in this industry, Tumika Cain. There is nothing more that I love in the whole writing process than getting my edits back after story development. It is a joy to read every single comment from you. I remember the very first time when I got my edits back I was a nervous wreck. Coffee had to talk to me to calm me down so I can step away for the ledge. I had over 150 comments, I was like,

"Damn, did I do anything right?" However, plenty of them were just positive things you liked about the story and the quotes. Thank you for everything. With your guidance and wisdom I was able to make TNAL the beautifully written story it is.

Shout-out to everyone at LDP. I pray that you guys continue to grow and prosper. As y'all know, I'm real big on quotes so I'll leave you all with this. "Without labor, nothing prospers." In order to become what you are meant to be you have to put actions into your dreams so they can become a reality. Keep grinding and let nothing or no one stand in your way to bigger and better things.

Adia Stribling, Yolanda Powell, Jessica Pitts, Pashion Allen, Pamela Ward and Kim Leblanc are just a few of the readers who I know stuck with me from start to finish. Thank you. Ladies. for loving the journey of Keyz and Shaunie just as much as I did.

Thank you to all the readers who took time to download and read my series. It is because of you I kept writing this series. It is because of your Facebook posts and inbox messages that I was able to keep moving forward and write it to completion. I couldn't let y'all down. I hope y'all enjoy the finale. #TNAL.

Notes: Please take a moment to show your support by leaving a short review.

Nikki Tee

Chapter 1

Nowadays, there's no honor, no loyalty. Only drama. Your friend today can be your enemy tomorrow.

-Unknown

Keyz

I stared into the eyes of the nigga who betrayed me and our team. After Rayne's warning, I knew it was someone close to me, but nothing could prepare me for this. Coming face to face with my betrayer. An emotion I registered distantly threatened to weaken my resolve of getting rid of the threat. However, my thirst for vengeance wouldn't be denied. The phantom pain from the hurtful betrayal gave way to a rising inferno of rage and my blood began to boil, the pain fueling my growing rage. He looked at me with a cauldron of emotions in his deceitful eyes. One emotion I easily recognized. *How come I never saw the envy that lived there before?* But then I remembered all the times I thought I saw something, but dismissed it easily. Well, I wouldn't make that mistake twice. Fool me once, shame on you. Fool me twice, shame on me. Pushing back the fondness I once held for him and any memories that I held of us as young'uns, I pulled the trigger with no regrets. *Pow!* The sound of the shot and a grunt from the bitch nigga on the floor echoed in the empty room.

Just as I pulled the trigger, Thugga knocked my hand away. The action caused my aim to waver from the intended target area of the head. Instead, the bullet hit Qwan's chest area. Blood immediately began oozing on the floor. Ignoring the painfully pitiful sounds that emitted from him, I reflexively turned my heater on Thugga. My trust level was real low.

"Whoa, Whoa, my nigga." With his 9mm still in his right hand, Thugga held up both hands like he was surrendering.

"Fuck is you doing knocking my muthafucking hand away?" I barked out at him while keeping my piece trained on him and one eye on Qwan, who was holding his hand over his gunshot wound. Thugga's interference caused my anger to spike a notch.

"That nigga might not be the only one involved. Before you put his lights out, we gotta find out who all is involved." He kept still and his eyes were unblinking as he looked at me. His non-threatening posture put me somewhat at ease. "If the noise that nigga is making is any indication, we ain't got much time." While he spoke, he maintained eye contact and stayed relaxed.

I realized that if Thugga was involved with this bullshit, he would have shot me when he came in behind me. He had the perfect time to eliminate me then. I dropped my hand to my side and turned all my attention to Qwan's ole bitch ass. As much shit as he talked about being real and the team this and that, one would have never known he was a traitor.

"You don't have that much time, so get to talking, my nigga," I said to him.

Qwan allowed his greed and envy to finally show in his eyes. The full force of it surprised me, because the niggas on my team eat just as good as me. It fucked with my head that he would turn on me and the team. Thoughts of why he would betray us fluttered in my mind for a moment. I thought we were all solid. Maybe other members on my team were feeling dissatisfied with the way shit was being ran. Shaking my head, I pushed the confusion away and shelved the why questions for later.

"Fuck..." He coughed up blood and it spewed over his face. "...you," he said with a smirk. The look told me he had info.

"No, nigga, fuck you. Hoe ass 'round here plotting and scamming and shit against your own fucking peoples." Thugga charged forward, but I pulled him back.

I used my gun to scratch my head. "Fuck me, huh?" My voice was laced with sarcasm. I knew it was useless to threaten him with bodily harm, he was smart enough to know that he wasn't leaving here alive. Torturing him wasn't gon' do shit but tire my ass out, plus the fool was barely breathing. "How about this?" I walked slowly toward him, one would think I was taking a stroll in the park. "Remember my Uncle Mike's dog, Rocco?" I asked in an eerily calm tone. His eyes widened in recognition, but he remained quiet. Rocca was known for his viciousness. "Yeah, I see you remember him. I might just grab your ma and let him have his way with her. Then, I'll grab your lil' girl and sell her on the black market. That's awful from what I hear. Let's not forget your girl. It's such a shame what happens to beautiful women who get addicted to heroin." I allowed him to hear how true my words rung. He knew how ruthless I could be. "Hahahaha. The possibilities are endless."

Kneeling down to his level, I looked him square in the eyes. I wanted to gauge his reaction. "Imma ask one time and one time only. I would hate to follow through with those things to your family." Qwan could be stubborn, but I was tenacious. He knew my words weren't threats but promises.

He seemed to be indecisive for a mere second. Then, he gave an imperceptible nod.

"Is there anyone from my team and crew who been plotting with you?"

"No." He gasped.

Well, at least I wouldn't have to put down anymore niggas that I fucked with. "So, who masterminded this shit and got your fake ass to flip sides? I don't give a fuck about the whys. I want the whos." Qwan was too hotheaded to sit down long enough to plot and strategize. Someone sold him a pipe dream and he bought it.

Qwan's eyelids began to droop and his breathing was shallow. I slapped him across the face to get him up. "Not yet, my nigga. You got an eternity to rest. Who muthafucka?"

Blood seeped from his chest and trickled from his mouth. "King." The name rung a bell. I remembered many niggas who thought they ran the city and called themselves King, but one King in particular stood out. He ran the majority of the city years ago and had it on lock before I took over. That year, the streets of New Orleans bled red and the residents were fearful of leaving their homes, not wanting to get caught up in the crossfire. The murder rate made history as we fought over territory. Eventually, his army of goons fell and he fled the city.

"D. King?" I asked and Qwan nodded.

Then, I remembered my conversation with Briggs in the interrogation room after the first shoot-out me and Thugga was involved in.

"A high speed chase with bullets flying that ended up causing an accident and putting a five-year-old in a coma is hardly what I would call a random shooting," the detective with Briggs said.

"I could care less what you would call it. If you aren't charging my client with any bogus charges, we're leaving. Time is money and you just cost us two hours. Stop harassing my clients or I will be forced to file charges against you and this god forsaken department," my attorney said indignantly. "Mr. Jones, let's go." Wainwright snatched his briefcase from the table.

I got up to follow my attorney out the door. As I passed by that crooked ass cop, Briggs, that nigga jumped in my face and whispered in a voice that couldn't be heard by anyone but me.

"This isn't over. My boss gon' take you down. The real king is taking over the streets of the N.O."

I looked at the detective who was seated at the far end of the table. Keeping my voice down, I looked back at Briggs' crooked ass. "Man, get the fuck out of here with that dumb shit. Now you want to take me down. Nigga, yo ass was working for me," I told him.

"Look here, lil' nigga, I don't work for nobody, I work for the dollars," he said with a smirk. Let him and whoever he now worked for come for me, they would get dealt with.

I came back to the present when I heard Thugga's voice. "Let's finish this shit and go."

I stood up and aimed my gun at Qwan's head. "Time to meet your maker. Keep the fires of hell burning, 'cause your conspirator will be joining you soon." I pulled the trigger and watched as blood and brain matter exploded from the impact of the bullet. Having known Qwan for many years, I should feel some kinda way about ending his existence. But after thinking about all the bullshit I went through because of his conniving, scheming ass, taking his life seemed fitting. He would have taken mine in a second, so I was only returning the favor. It was either him or me.

At the sound of approaching footsteps, Thugga and I turned with our weapons ready to bust heads. Rayne and Hassan burst through the room with their guns in the same position as ours. We all lowered our guns. The duo looked at the body and then back at me and Thugga, seeking answers. Qwan was unrecognizable.

"It was Qwan all along. He plotted with D. King to take back control of the city," Thugga explained to them.

Shaking his head, Rayne looked at the body and spat on the floor. "Loyalty is so hard to find." Then he turned to Hassan. "Let this be your warning. Stay real or get put down." Hassan merely nodded, taking Rayne's words for what they were.

"Go to the truck and get the kerosene from the trunk. We got to burn this bitch down. Too much DNA and shit from us that could be used against us," I ordered Hassan.

He turned and walked out the room to do as he was told. The shrill ringing from a cell phone pierced the room. We all looked over in the direction of Qwan's remains. I stalked over and fished out the cell phone from his pocket. It was then that I noticed the phone wasn't his usual phone but a burner. I looked at his screen and saw it was King. I swiped my finger across the screen and put it to my ear.

"What's taking you so long? Yo ass was supposed to be in and out," he said.

"Qwan can't come to the phone right now. He's in his final resting place."

There was a moment of silence before a peel of sinister laughter erupted from the caller's mouth. "Well, well, well. If it isn't the man of the hour, Keyz himself. You finally put two and two together. It took you long enough."

His words grated on my nerves, because it did take me a minute to get to the bottom of this shit with all my distractions. "It ain't gon' take me long to find your hoe ass. Just know I'm gunning for you."

"Bold words, my friend. It doesn't have to be a war again. Just step back and leave town."

"Nigga, you must be mental talking fucking stupid. This is *my* mothafucking city. I run this and there isn't a place you can hide from me now that I know it's you. Pussy ass nigga scheming like bitches. Face me like a G." I wasn't one to hide behind another nigga. My enemies were going to see me coming.

"We'll see about that," King said before hanging up.

After I hung up the phone, I looked at my dawgs. "It's that bitch ass King, just like Qwan said."

"I guess last time we went to war with his ass wasn't enough. Bitch made nigga left town with his ass in his hand. What the fuck that bitch nigga had to say?" Thugga asked.

"He wants control of the city. Funny thing tho,' he thought I was gone step down and let him move in." I shook my head. "You already know it ain't going down like that."

My mind went into overdrive as I thought about how to lure him out. I was tired of the cat and mouse games. "Check his phone for contacts and anything else that's useful. Try to track that last number." I handed the phone to Rayne.

Rayne took the phone and put it in his pocket. "You know I got that covered." I nodded at him.

Hassan came back in the room with three cans of kerosene. "Yo, let's do this and roll out. I'm getting antsy as fuck around here."

I took the kerosene and walked over to Qwan's body. "Rayne, you do the downstairs area. Thugga you do the perimeter around the house. Hassan, keep watch. Don't light it up until everybody is outside."

They left out the room to complete their directives. I opened the can and doused the corpse. Immediately, the fumes from the chemical filled the room. Looking out the window, I saw my boys standing by the curb. Fishing in my pocket, I took out my lighter. Moving a safe distance back, I put the can outside the door.

I took the rubber band off a roll of money in my pocket. Flicking the ignition of the lighter, I adjusted the flame to high. Then, double knotting the rubber band, I placed it over the bottom of the lighter to the top of the switch. Stepping back, I threw the lighter toward Qwan's body. Before the lighter landed, the flames swallowed the body.

Once I was out the bedroom, I grabbed the kerosene and left a trail of it on the stairs. Quickly completing my task, I joined my boys outside. "Light it up," I told Hassan. He lit a match and threw it at the house. The spark had the house going up in flames.

We didn't stay around to make sure it burned. It was only a matter of time before the fire department came. Plus, we had been at the house for about fifteen minutes and that was more than enough.

Once inside the car, we sped off. From the back seat, Hassan asked, "So, what's next?"

"We find that nigga, King, and kill his ass once and for all," Thugga said.

From the front seat, I nodded my head not looking back at them, but keeping my eyes forward. "Now, we prepare for war."

There was no way I was going to just start looking for King and his crew with guns ablaze and without strategizing all angles. Failing to prepare was preparing to fail. My gut told me that this was the last time King and I would battle it out. I had too much to lose and I just got my family back. In this, I couldn't fail.

Chapter 2

The highest spiritual quality, the noblest property of mind a man can have is this of loyalty...a man with no loyalty in him, with no sense of love or reverence or devotion due to something outside and above his poor daily life, with its pains and pleasures, profits and losses, is as evil a case as man can be.

-Algernon Charles Swimburne

Shaunie

The door to the day care center chimed as the last parent walked out with their child and Nikki walked behind them to lock the door. It had been two weeks since the opening of Kid's Kingdom Academy. Business was already booming. All available spaces were filled and I had seven workers, plus myself and Nikki. The other workers were allowed to leave once most of the kids got picked up by their parents, leaving me and Nikki to get ready for next week.

"Girl, let's get this place cleaned up so I can go," Nikki said. It was a Friday and Nikki was hyped about going out.

I picked Keira up and we all walked to my office. "You running home to Thugga?" I asked with a smirk on my face. After Thugga cheated one time too many and refused to move out when Nikki ended their relationship, Nikki moved in with me. Since me and Keyz got back together, Nikki moved out. She claimed she didn't want to impose on us while we worked on our differences. The old house had too many bad memories for me, so we decided to sell it and move Keyz into my new home. Our new home.

Beside me, I heard teeth smacking. "Girl, fuck a Thugga! Bitch, you know I don't live with his ass no more. Hell, I wouldn't spit on that bitch if he was on fire."

Laughter involuntary escaped my mouth as she went in on him. Surprisingly, she didn't go back to Thugga when she moved out. Nikki finally thought of herself first and got her own apartment.

"I'm just messing with you. Damn. Are you going out with Trey again?" Trey is a guy Nikki met a few weeks back at Taco Bell while making a food run for the daycare workers. The fact that she was entertaining another man was surprising. She and Thugga had been together since she was a teenager. The progress she was making attempting to move on was remarkable.

Nikki plopped down in the chair with a smile on her face. "Yes. I am."

"You sitting there with a Kool-aid smile on your face. You must like him." While I talked to her, I balanced Keira on my lap and put this week's payments in the money bag. I looked up when I noticed Nikki was quiet. "Well, do you?"

She smacked her teeth. "To be honest, I really don't know. I like chilling with him, but as far as it being anything deeper than that, I don't know." When she finished speaking, she looked away.

"It's okay if you..." I stopped talking when Keira started patting me repeatedly after I didn't answer her when she first tried to get my attention. I looked down at her. "What did I tell you about patting people? Big girls use their words." Stopping mid-air, she put her hand down.

"Mommy, I wanna play with iPad." She pointed to the desk drawer where I kept her iPad during working hours.

All she wanted to do was play on her electronics. I didn't want her to become absorbed in it, so I shook my head no. "How about you color in your coloring book? You can play on your iPad later." I opened my drawer, retrieved her coloring book and crayons, and gave them to her.

"Okay mommy. I'm going color with my pink." Hopping off my lap, she took her things. "I love pink. Princesses wear pink." She babbled on as she settled herself on the floor next to my desk.

I watched her for a minute with an indulgent smile on my face. Her mood had improved significantly since Keyz and I decided to make things work. She wasn't as clingy and whiny anymore, except when she wanted her way and her daddy gave in to her.

"Girl, that lil' girl is spoiled rotten. It's gon' take one helluva dude to get her when she grows up."

I laughed at the thought of a dude trying to get with Keira. "Honey, she is going to be a spinster. Keyz ain't letting nobody near her."

"Between Keyz, Lil' Corey and Shaun, I feel sorry for any man that thinks they stand a chance with her.

I barely flinched when she mentioned Shaun's name. Even though Keyz and I decided to get back together and I didn't hold anything against an innocent like Shaun, it was still hard to talk about him. I didn't stop Keyz or Keira from spending time with him, but I needed time before I integrated him in my life. He deserved to be loved and a part of my family, so I had to get myself together so I didn't make him uncomfortable when he did come around.

For the time being, Keyz and Keira spent time with Shaun at Ms. Lynn's house. A few times they even slept over. It wasn't easy dealing with Keyz' baby situation. I struggled still with the acceptance of it. Especially considering my own son, who I aborted, would have been close to the same age. Every day he apologized for having his son on me, but I was slowly coming to terms with it. I almost lost my life over it and lost a job I loved. I didn't mind the losing the job part so much anymore. It was a blessing in disguise, because it forced me to pursue my dream of opening up my daycare center. I nodded my head in response to her statement.

"What are you wearing for your date?" I asked with a brittle smile, changing the topic.

Sensing my desire to drop the subject, she followed suit. "I don't know what I'm wearing, so let me get to my duties so I can have some time to find something," she said, standing to her feet.

"You know what? How about you take Keira and y'all get out of here?" My mom was waiting for me to drop her off to spend the night anyway."

When Keira heard she was going by my mom, she stood up and clapped her hands. "Yay. I get to stay with Granny."

We looked at Keira shaking her little butt as she hopped in circles in excitement. Chuckling at her antics, we got back to the matter at hand.

"Are you sure, Shaunie?"

"Yeah. It won't take me anytime to clean up. Y'all go ahead." I turned to Keira and held out my hands. "Come and give mommy a kiss. Auntie Nikki is going to bring you by granny." Keira launched herself into my arms and I held on tight. Moments like this fill me with so much joy. I inhaled her sweet scent that never failed to give me comfort. "See you later alligator," I said as I kissed her silky cheek.

"Afta while crocodile," she said in her toddler voice, that didn't allow her to pronounce all of the sounds in the words, before she kissed my cheek and ran to her auntie.

"Alright, boo. I'll call you tomorrow." Nikki grabbed her things. "Oh, don't forget we have brunch on Sunday with Stacy.

"I didn't forget," I said, playing it off, because I totally forgot. My friendship with Stacy had been strained the past few weeks because of what happened at the mall when she confessed to cheating on Killer. She was upset with how I reacted and I was upset that she even told me about it. It's not that I wasn't trying to be supportive of her when she needed someone to talk to. I loved my friend like a sister. But I just didn't want to be a part of it and now that I had the knowledge that it happened, I was a part of it and the burden was now mine too. A lot of friends were cool with knowing that their friends were creeping around, whether it was one time or many. I wasn't built that way. My loyalty was first and foremost to my friend, but I had to be around Killer. Having to laugh and smile in his face when I knew a secret that would hurt him seemed fake to me. And I knew firsthand the sting of betrayal.

Nikki laughed when she saw the look on my face. "I knew you forgot, so don't try to play it off, heifer."

I playfully pushed her arm. "Whatever! I invited Minnie. I hope y'all don't mind." Minnie was Keyz' friend Yuriah's wife, but we quickly bonded when we realized we had so much in common. We had a strong sense of family, we're loyal to a fault, and were driven to be successful in our own right, in spite of the fact our men had money. We were also all wrapped up and sprinkled with a dash of naivety, due to us being inexperienced in relationships.

"Girl, Minnie cool peeps."

We walked to the door and I hugged Nikki before she picked up Keira to head to the car. "Have fun on your date."

After they walked out the door, I locked it before I walked around the center and made sure everything was in place. Putting my earplugs in, old school jams filled my ears as I wiped down the toys and swept and mopped the floor. I could have hired someone to cook and clean for the center, but this was my passion and I took great joy in doing the simple jobs. As I worked in comfortable solitude and listened to the music, the love songs made me think about Keyz and my relationship. We were taking things slow, but we were definitely back together. With a smile spreading across my face, I stopped cleaning and fingered the gold heart locket he gave me the other day. He was so serious when he presented this gift to me. After getting a promise from me to never remove it, he said it represented how solid his love was for me. The heart symbolized our love and the gold symbolized how precious our love was. I tucked my necklace back inside my shirt and finished cleaning.

When I was done sterilizing everything, I did one last walk through the building. Satisfied that everything was ready for Monday, I gathered my things, set the alarm on the building and strolled to the parking lot.

As I walked to the car, a bad feeling started in the pit of my stomach and the feeling rose with each step away from the safety of the daycare building, making me nervous. I increased my pace to a brisk walk, but the feeling didn't fade. Fear gripped me and my senses heightened intensely, causing me to pick up every sound around me. When I heard a noise behind me, my nervousness bloomed into full blown panic. My heart rate accelerated *God I hope this is just my imagination.* Listening to my instincts, I sprinted to my car. I pressed the key fob to unlock the door. Just when I reached out to open the door, my hair was pulled from behind. The purse I was carrying fell to the ground and the contents spilled out. Not giving in to hysterics, I lifted my leg and kicked back with as much force as I could. Then I let loose a scream at the top of my lungs that could wake the dead. "Heeeeeeeelp!" The sun was just setting, so I was hoping people would still be out and about. Maybe someone would hear my cry for help and call the police. *Please, God, don't let my last moments on Earth be this, killed in a parking lot.*

"Oooowww fuck, you stupid bitch!" the assailant said, but didn't release my hair. Instead, he wrapped his forearm around my neck, choking me, instantly silencing my cry for help. I struggled to breathe with the tight grip he had. I groped at his arm and raked my nails into his flesh, drawing specks of blood. *At least if he kills me, there will be DNA,* the rational part of my brain that wasn't removed from reality thought. He began walking me backwards and I lurched forward using all of my weight to prevent him from carrying me away. I struggled against the assailant with all the might I could muster, but he outweighed me.

A punch to my side and a tighter hold on my neck weakened me further. I fought him off as long as I could, but being stronger, the man quickly overpowered me. His hand reached for my face and that was when I saw the white cloth. The smell of chloroform filled my senses. My struggles increased in self-preservation. Twisting and turning, I tried to get the cloth away from me, but the man holding me was stronger. As my lungs filled with the sweet sickly smell, the fight slowly drained out of me. My reflexes slowed down, but I was aware of calloused hands catching me before I fell. *Thank God Nikki took Keira with her earlier*, was my last thought before darkness swallowed me.

***

With a groan, I slowly came to my senses. My body felt heavy and my pounding head made me dizzy. As I struggled to sit up, the events that took place came back to me in a rush. My eyes popped open as wide as my still drugged mind would allow. I quickly looked around the unfamiliar room while climbing out the bed. The jerking on my hand forced me back when I got three feet from the bed. The kidnapper used manacles to handcuff me to the burglar bar on the window that was over the bed. The dark sky told me maybe a few hours had passed since I been here. With a pounding and heavy heart, I sat on the bed with my legs folded beneath me as I tried to think. I didn't scream for help just yet because I didn't want to alert the abductor that I was awake. I scanned the room for something close that I could use as a weapon. It seemed that he must have thought ahead, because the room was emptied of everything but the bed, dresser, and a floor lamp that was too far for me to reach it.

I placed my head in my hand as desolation threatened to overwhelm me. The rattling of the shackle around my wrist must have informed my captor that I was up and about, because no sooner than I moved my hand, did the door open and he walked in.

When I looked up, I came face to face with the man who snatched me away from my family. He came farther inside of the room and my eyes widened in surprise at the sight of someone who was easily recognizable to me. The surprise was quickly replaced with confusion when I had a moment to think of reasons why he would feel the need to kidnap me. I gasped in shock and my breathing accelerated

"No. No, this isn't happening," I muttered out loud. Feelings of betrayal filled me until it felt as if I would explode. *It was all a lie! Every look and tender touch was a lie!* Why else would I be locked inside a room, restrained? I felt foolish for falling for all his sweet words, but above all the other emotions, I felt anger at myself for not seeing the truth sooner.

He walked in the room with a twisted smirk on his face like he took pleasure in my confusion and pain. I wanted to run up on him and smash the look off his face, but I didn't know what he had planned for me, so I tried to keep my cool. Panic and acting without thinking had no place here, if I wanted to know his end game and leave here alive.

"Well, well, well. I see you are finally awake. You look a little worse for wear," he said as he stepped closer to the bed with his hands stuffed in his pockets.

I wanted to wrap the chain around his throat and squeeze until his light skinned ass turned blue. "What do you want?"

He stopped beside the bed and stood next to me. Slowly, he removed his hand and trailed his knuckle down my cheek. I turned my head away from his repulsive touch. The action amused him, because he laughed out loud.

"Don't worry. I don't want you personally. I just want to use you to get to Keyz." My eyebrows scrunched down in confusion. *What does this have to do with Keyz? How does he know either one of us?* Upon seeing his face, my mind immediately went to a more personal connection not involving Keyz, but his words proved me wrong. "You are just collateral damage. It's such a shame I couldn't get that little baby girl of his. Now that shit would have been epic. That's enough to break a grown man."

22

At the mention of my daughter, I forgot all about my safety. Red clouded my vision as rage consumed me. He fucked up talking about my daughter.

"You fucking bastard!" I threw my leg out and it connected with his knee. He bent over and tried to jump back, but I hurled myself on his back and began pounding my fist like a hammer. I knew I shouldn't have antagonized him, but fuck it. Clearly, he was going to kill me. He had another thing coming if he thought I was going to lie down, roll over, and accept it.

Chapter 3

You don't earn loyalty in a day. You earn loyalty day-by-day.
-Jeffrey H. Gitomer

Keyz

"Yo, Shaunie!" I yelled as I entered the front door. Walking into the house, I peeled off my sweat soaked t-shirt and threw it and my ballistic vest on the floor. I walked to the master suite when I realized she wasn't home yet. Her car keys weren't in the tray on the foyer table and her car wasn't parked in the driveway or the garage. I called her phone, but it went to voicemail so I left a message. I hadn't been home since last night when me and the crew laid the trap to catch the rat. After torching the place, me and the fellows laid low. Even though Qwan said no one else was involved, I didn't want to take a chance of a nigga following me home and retaliating where my family laid their heads.

It's been a whole day since I saw my girl. We spoke on the phone last night, but ain't nothing like being with her. Since I left the trap house, I had been feeling some type of way, but contributed the feelings surfacing to killing Qwan's bitch ass. After all the shit we been through as boys and a team, this nigga fucked over me for what? That question was one I would have to live with not knowing the answer to. At the end of the day, the why didn't even matter because betrayal was betrayal. This nigga was laughing in my face and sitting at my table to eat, but at the same time plotting my downfall.

I hopped in the shower to wash off the grime and blood before my girl and daughter came home. Even though she knew that I got down and dirty sometimes, I didn't expose her to that life. I damn sure didn't want her asking me questions either. *I gotta get rid of that vest*, I muttered to myself. Once I got out of the shower, I dried off and brushed my teeth over the sink. When I looked in the mirror,

I saw the bruises on my chest. The reflection revealed bluish black circular contusions from the impact of the bullets through the vest. *So much for avoiding questions from Shaunie's ass.* She was going to spazz out when she saw my chest. Examining the discolorations, I poked and prodded until it made me flinch. If getting shot in the chest with a bulletproof vest hurt like this shit, then I hated to know what it felt like without one. I didn't know how Thugga dealt with the pain when he got shot four times in the chest and stomach area.

Rambling through the cabinet under the bathroom sink, I found some witch hazel and ibuprofen for the pain and bruising. Shaunie was going to be pissed that I made a mess of her neatly organized cabinet. Then, I went into the bedroom and threw on some jeans, a tee shirt, and some tennis shoes before I went downstairs to wait for my two favorite girls to come home. I was happy as fuck my girl gave me another chance. She put a nigga through it before she took me back. I was still having a hard time believing she fucked around with another nigga, but I had to let that shit slide, 'cause I did a lot worse. Every night I was beating that pussy up. She ain't gonna even remember him after a while. I wanted it to go back to how we used to be. It was me and Shaunie. We didn't have any doubts who we belonged to. This time, I was going to do right by her. Bitches these days couldn't even get me to spit on them if they were on fire. Hell, my dick wouldn't even twitch unless it was for my bae.

While channel surfing the sport channels, I couldn't seem to relax. Instead of the tension in my body draining away, my muscles grew tighter. The bad vibes I had been feeling increased and I couldn't shake it. I had waited for over an hour. Picking up my phone, I called Shaunie's phone three times and all calls had gone unanswered. At first, her not picking up didn't bother me because it was a late Friday evening and I knew she usually be busy at work. But the feeling of uneasiness didn't fade and those feelings multiplied when her bodyguard didn't answer a few minutes ago. *Man, this shit with King got me tripping*, I muttered. I dialed Nikki's number and waited for her to answer.

"Hello."

"You with Shaunie?" I asked, getting straight to the point.

"Well hey to your rude ass too." I heard her smack her teeth and I'm sure she rolled her eyes too. She was still giving me a hard time for what happened between me and her girl. I was glad that Shaunie had such a loyal friend who was there for her when she needed someone, but Nikki ass had better fall the fuck back and worry about Thugga.

"On the real, Shaunie ain't answering her phone. Where is she?"

Her sharp intake of breath told me she heard the seriousness in my voice. The last time I called her looking for Shaunie, she was upstairs in the bathroom. She had accidently ODed. "She was at the center. I left early with Keira. Shaunie asked me to drop Keira off at her mom's house while she stayed behind to clean up the place."

I turned around and walked out the door with my phone to my ear, headed to my car. "Okay. I'm on my way there." I hung up without waiting for a reply. Something drove me to get to the daycare center as fast as I could. I floored the gas as I raced there. Several times, I called her and Jontrell, her bodyguard, but they didn't answer. *Maybe I am being paranoid*, I tried to convince myself. My gut churned because it was telling me something went down or was about to go down.

The first thing I noticed when I turned on the street of the daycare was the flashing lights of the police cars and I heard the sirens from an ambulance as I pulled up. *Damn, baby. Please be alright,* I said like a prayer, hoping I was being paranoid. When I got closer, I saw the yellow crime tape surrounding the area around a black sedan that looked like it belonged to the bodyguard. The only thing that calmed be down was all of the activity took place several yards away from Shaunie's building and the adjacent parking lot of the building. I prayed that she was okay and safely tucked away inside. But I wasn't so sure of that.

I sat in my car for a few minutes to observe the scene before I got out the car and mingled with the other bystanders to watch the events unfold. The officers walked over to several people standing about and seemed to be questioning them for information on what happened. Once I got closer, I realized that the car did belong to Jontrell. "Yo, what happened?" I asked some random chick who was standing there watching. I needed info because I knew this shit couldn't have been random.

"I dunno know. I heard sirens and came to see what all the noise was about. They say some dude was found inna car," she said while smacking on her gum.

"Anybody else with him?" I pressed for more details.

"Nope. Just him."

Playing it off, I shook my head. "That's fucked up." When the single body of the bodyguard was removed from the car and placed in the black bag, I walked back to my car. I drove around the block to the back street that opened to the parking lot of the daycare center. Sure enough, my girl's car was parked in her spot. Relief made my shoulders sag and I exhaled a lung full of air I didn't realize I was holding.

My relief was short lived when I parked next to her, on the driver side, and saw her purse on the ground with the contents scattered around the parking lot. It was the only evidence that confirmed my worse fear. King snatched my girl. That nigga knew my greatest weakness. It wasn't a secret how I felt about Shaunie. When me and King first fought over territory seven years ago, a lot of people didn't know me and Shaunie was rocking like that, so he didn't know to use her.

"Fuck!" I pounded the steering wheel before I pulled my cell from my pocket and called Thugga. Not giving him a chance to say anything, I told him the situation. "That bitch nigga got Shaunie," I said through the speaker.

"Where's Nikki?" he quickly asked. I heard him gasp a little through the phone. He and Nikki still weren't together. From what Shaunie told me, they may not get back together, ever. Nikki was officially through. She didn't even answer his calls. Everything involving Lil Thugga was mediated by Thugga's mama, Ms. Rochelle. Despite all the bullshit they went through and he put her through, Thugga loved her to death. He would never want anything to happen to her and I knew if something ever did he would be destroyed.

"She good. I just got off the phone with her," I said, taking a pause from my own worries to reassure my nigga about his girl

"Man, let's meet up and plan someth…"

I knew what he was trying to say was probably the best route to take, but I couldn't stand idly by and just wait. The longer I waited to go after my girl, the slimmer her chances were of making it out alive. As it is, I didn't know what the fuck he was doing to her. If I had to die getting her away from King, then it would be the last thing I did. My life wasn't shit compared to hers and I didn't have a problem sacrificing it.

"Fuck that shit. I gotta get my girl. Imma text you the location. Y'all niggas meet me there with the rest of the crew," I said cutting him off and hanging up the call. I opened up the Tagg app on my phone and pulled up the chip that was assigned to Shaunie. Thank God for foresight A few weeks ago, I gave her a locket as a gift. Unbeknownst to her, behind the picture of our family, was a dog chip that tracked her activity and location. My mom had a matching necklace and my son and daughter had bracelets. I wasn't on no stalker type shit, trying to keep track of her whereabouts. A man in my position can't be too careful with the people he cherished. Niggas wouldn't hesitate to use my family to get to me. I need to prepare in the event it ever happened.

The red dot pinpointed a location that was about twenty minutes out. Between the time it had been since she had been grabbed and the time it would take me to get there, anything could happen. I texted the location to Thugga. Not having a minute to lose, I quickly used my key for the center and opened the door. The alarm chirped and I put in the code to deactivate it. Jogging to her office, I sat in the chair and pulled up the surveillance feed for the cameras that my security people installed around the building. I wanted to see what I was up against when I went to the site where King had taken her. The video showed the one assailant grabbing Shaunie from behind and attempted to drag her away. I saw her put up the best fight she could, but I didn't have time to appreciate her efforts.

Once I scoped out the videos, I hopped back in my car and checked my 9mm. I grabbed my spare magazine from the glove compartment and put it in my pocket. Satisfied that I had adequate protection, I started my car and drove like a maniac. In the race of time to save my girl, the other motorists seemed to be driving slow as snails. Traffic laws and the police never crossed my mind as I raced against time to get Shaunie back. My impatience had me blowing my horn and cussing them out. I bypassed all the red lights and stop signs I encountered. I think I may have caused an accident or two, but I didn't give a fuck. Hell, I didn't even give a fuck that I was riding armed. The only thing I cared about was getting to my girl before King did irrevocable damage to her or killed her outright, if he hadn't already.

Chapter 4

Loyalty means nothing unless it has at its heart the absolute principle of self-sacrifice.

-Woodrow Wilson

Shaunie

The tugging on my hair made it hard for me to keep my hold on his back and punch him at the same time. I knew I wouldn't win against him, but I was trying to beat his back in. His grip tightened further and he slung me off him. With a bounce that knocked the wind out of me, I landed on the bed on my back, but that didn't stop me. I attempted to get up, but the smack to my face made me see stars and dazed me for a minute. Holding my stinging cheek, I glared at him. If looks could kill, he would be dead and I wouldn't need a weapon.

"Now, bitch, I tried to be nice to your ass, but you pushing me. Sit your muthafucking ass down now."

Chest heaving, I sat down on the bed and folded my arms. "Fuck you, nigga!"

He stepped closer and grabbed a strand of my hair. "Such a feisty lil' thing. I wonder if that pussy is just as hot," he said as he rubbed his fingers up and down the length of my hair.

I jerked my head away from his hand and turned away. "What do you want? Why am I here?"

With more force than necessary, he turned my head back to face him, while applying pressure that I was sure would leave bruises. "I'm going to ransom you back to Keyz, while sending him piece by piece of your body. And when he comes to pick up the rest of you, I'm going to kill him and take back the city that rightfully belongs to me." I couldn't believe I was being put through all this craziness because this mad man wanted control over the city. The worth of my life was reduced to a piece of land.

My eyes widened and my heart began to beat faster in my chest at his confession of what he planned to do to me because of his beef with Keyz over territory. Trembles racked my frame at the implication of what he had planned for me. Not showing the fear that he just instilled in me by his words, I lifted my face and stared at him defiantly.

"You may as well…" I began to tell him, but the sound of keys jingling stopped me and I strained my ears to hear.

Simultaneously, both of our heads spun toward the door. Footsteps echoed through the house and a voice called out. I didn't know if it was his accomplice or my savior. My nerves were shot at this point. He turned toward me and leaned over to whisper in my ear. "Don't scream or what I have in store for you will be ten times worse."

I cocked my head to the side and rolled my eyes. This dude must have thought I was stupid. He just told me he was going to kill me and now he was telling me not to scream. The fact that he wanted me to be quiet let me know he didn't expect anyone else.

I watched as he slowly and quietly cracked open the door. As he pushed open the door, I heard the footsteps approaching closer and closer. When he slipped out the room, leaving the door open, I let loose the loudest scream I could. I was certain I wasn't leaving here alive, so I wasn't taking it lying down.

"Heeeeeeeeelp!" I screamed at the top of my lungs.

The footsteps drew closer and faster. Pulse racing, I prayed it was someone coming to help me. A figure appeared in the doorway. I guess God didn't answer my prayers because Dam stood there staring at me.

"What the hell!" He walked near me, but I backed away from him. "Shaunie, what the hell is going on here?" he asked me with concern in his voice.

"Get the fuck away from me! Don't act like you don't know what the fuck is going on! This shit was all planned from the beginning."

He turned to me with deep shock in his eyes. Dam knelt on the bed next to me and began tugging on the chains, but it wouldn't come loose. "What are you talking about? This is my family's property. I told you I was the overseer." He talked while he worked on getting the chains off.

"Exactly! I was kidnapped and now I'm here with your brother." At the mention of his brother, he stilled. His act was so believable, but I wasn't going to be naïve again.

He looked frantically around the room. "We have to get you out of here. I am going to look for something to break these chains. I'll be right back."

I grabbed his forearm to keep him from leaving. "Wait. You're going to just leave me here." I didn't trust him, but I was going to use him to get out of here.

"Listen, Damien is as ruthless as they come. He is going to kill you." He placed his hand on my cheek and looked me in the eyes. "I promise I will be right back."

I nodded my head as I pulled on my chain, wondering if it were possible he really *didn't* know about all of this going down. The door creaked and Damien walked into the room.

"If it isn't my baby brother. Imagine my surprise when I found out you were fucking a drug dealer's girl." He laughed. It sounded so maniacal that it sent a chill down my spine. "I didn't think you had it in you," he told Dam.

Dam got off the bed and walked toward his brother. "What the fuck man? What kind of shit did you get into now?" He pushed his brother, making him stumble back. "I'm letting her go." He searched the drawers looking for the keys to release me. "Whatever problem you have with me, this is between us."

"This doesn't have shit to do with your square ass. This has everything to do with Keyz, her nigga."

While they talked, I inched off the bed and edged my way closer to them. I had no plan for what to do. But if they started to fight, I was going to help Dam. Stick with the devil you know.

"It doesn't matter. Give me the key to release her," Dam told his brother, holding out his hand like he thought his brother was going to really give him the key that easily.

Damien took a gun from his back and pointed it at me. "The only thing I'm releasing involving her is a bullet."

My heart raced and I almost passed out from holding my breath. I slowly walked back until my legs hit the back of the bed.

"Damien, calm down. You are not thinking straight. She is innocent. She has nothing to do with you and this Keyz character," Dam said. He was trying to keep his gun toting brother focused on him.

"Nigga, I can't believe we share the same parents. You are so fucking weak. It's sickening."

The rattle of my chain must have drawn their attention because they both turned to me. I stopped my movement.

"There's nowhere to go," Damien said keeping his gun leveled on me with his finger on the trigger.

Abruptly, Dam tackled him and they both fell to the floor with his brother beneath him. They tussled for supremacy, toppling over the lamp and knocking into the dresser. I had nowhere to go, but that didn't stop me from continuing to tug the chains in the hope that it would give way. Getting the upper hand, Dam snatched the gun by the barrel, and twisted it away. *Pow!* The sound of the gun going off made me freeze again. It was so close to me that the noise nearly deafened me. I quickly turned again and saw Dam's body jerk back. My mouth opened in disbelief as his body fell to the floor not even two feet from where I stood.

"Oh my God, Dam." I dropped down to the floor next to him. My hands trembled and I didn't know what to do. "What did you do?" I asked in a broken and low, but accusatory tone. I looked up at the man that may have very well killed his brother.

Damien got up off the floor. "It was an accident. I didn't mean for that to happen." He started pacing, smoking gun still in his hands.

I looked back down to Dam. "Call for help!" I placed my hand on the chest wound to try to stop the flow. In seconds, my hand was drenched in his blood. The speed in which his blood seeped from his wound sent me in panic mode. I removed my hand and crawled to his head. I placed his head in my lap and stared in his eyes that were slowly becoming glossy. All I could do is look down at him with disbelief and sadness in my eyes.

The lunatic who was pacing the floor didn't appear to hear my cry for help. He began to mumble to himself while wearing the floor out. I looked up at him with disgust. If I wasn't so upset about the events that had just played out and Dam's head wasn't in my lap, I would get up and knock the shit out of him. The whole situation was just senseless. All over territory that didn't truly belong to him or Keyz.

"I didn't know," Dam gasped, "my brother had you." He struggled to get oxygen into his lungs. The task of breathing seemed to get harder and harder with each breath he exhaled.

I gripped the sheet hanging on the bed and dragged it to me. Once the sheet was off the bed, I balled it up and placed it on his chest, applying pressure. "It's okay. Don't worry about that right now."

"It was real." Dam coughed as he tried to speak. "All of it was real." Blood spewed from his mouth.

"Sssshhhh, don't talk." I caressed his face. Tears clouded my vision. My distrust of him vanished in the face of the tragedy that befell him. He battled his brother trying to keep me safe. I couldn't believe that a man I was intimate with and had some feeling for was lying before me bloody at the hands of his own brother. Helplessness almost overwhelmed me. I couldn't do anything to help him but hold him.

His hand traveled to my hand that was touching his face. When he reached his destination, he cupped my hand with his. I moved my fingers and interlocked our hands together. Then I brought them to my lips, kissing them.

He attempted a smile, but it was weak, just as weak as his grip on my fingers. "I love you." His gasps came faster.

The tears I tried to hold back broke from the dam and I sobbed. "I love you too." My heart broke just a little bit in that moment. I was so caught up in my emotions over Keyz that I hadn't realized I'd started to love Dam, too. My love for him wasn't all consuming. It was more of a gentle and safe love. But it was love nevertheless.

Blood soaked through the sheet. Dam gasped and gurgled with a rattling noise. That telltale rattling noise told me that death was almost upon him. I held his hand with his head on my lap as I watched, helplessly, as he took his last breath.

Damien stopped pacing. "No, no, no!" he screamed. He stopped in front of his brother's body.

I looked up to see him hitting himself on the head with the gun. *I wished he would just kill himself.* I didn't say the words out loud, but my eyes conveyed my thought as surely as if I had spoken them.

"This is all your fault." *Uh, excuse me! How the hell is this my fault when I didn't have the gun?! He sounds like a damn fool!*

I stood up with my fist balled at my side. "You should have called for help instead of acting like a fucking lunatic. Now Dam is dead, because of you. You killed your brother. You wanted Keyz so bad. But your brother paid the price." My chest rose and fell rapidly in anger.

He raised his weapon. I had no one to protect me this time. With certainty, my moment to die had come. "You are going to pay for this."

Backing up slowly, I climbed on the bed.

"I'll get to Keyz another way, but you have to die for this."

I realized this man was unstable. He blamed me for his brother's death when I wasn't the person with the gun. Closing my eyes and holding my breath, I waited for him to pull the trigger and this nightmare to stop.

Pow! Pow! Pow!

When he finally pulled the trigger, I tensed and braced for the impact.

Nikki Tee

Chapter 5

Where there is loyalty, weapons are of no use.

-Paulo Coelho

Keyz

I let off round after round. King dropped his gun and slowly fell to the floor. Seeing him pointing a gun at my lady brought out the beast in me. Real quick, I surveyed the room. King's figure had blocked the view of the room when I first walked up behind him, but I now had a clear line of vision of the entire space and when my eyes landed on another body, it shocked the hell out of me. Near the edge of the bed, on the floor, lay the body of the dude Shaunie was fucking with. *What the fuck was this nigga doing here?* I didn't know why he was here, but as soon as we got out of here I was going to find out. Stepping over the bodies and the blood that was slowly forming a small puddle, I made my way to the bed where Shaunie sat with her knees tucked under her and her eyes closed tight. The scene of seeing King aiming the gun at her and the fear I felt radiating from her was a sight that I was sure would cause me sleepless nights in the months ahead.

After jumping in my car, I drove here as fast as I could, barely stopping at red lights. The guilt over failing her by allowing this to happen and not reaching her in time made me move faster than I ever had. I stopped in front of Shaunie, having never been so glad to see her in my life. Reaching out a hand, I lifted her chin and pulled her face up to me, but she still didn't open her eyes.

"I got you, bae," I softly spoke to her. This experience must have been frightening to her and I needed to do everything in my power to keep her calm. With my fingers, I gently stroked her chin.

At the sound of my voice and touch, she finally opened her eyes. Her beautiful hazel eyes were filled with unshed tears.

"Keyz!! Thank God. I was so scared." She wrapped her arms around my shoulders and buried her head in my neck. Putting the gun down on the bed between us, I moved my head down, inhaled her scent before placing a kiss on her head. The tears she had been holding were sliding down my neck as she sobbed quietly while I held her. We took comfort from each other as we clung.

"Sssshhhh." I pulled back from her. Brushing her hair back with my hand, I leaned over and chastely kissed her lips. Her tears continued to fall and her shoulders jerked as she noiselessly cried. My lips pressed against her cheek, brow, and eyelids in gentle kisses that caused me to taste the salt of her tears. I wanted to hurry and leave, but I knew she needed a moment to get herself together to recover. Trying to be there for my girl, I was oblivious to anything else, except meeting her needs.

Her sobs subsided and she slowly raised her head. She opened her mouth to speak, but her eyes shifted to the right of me. As I turned around, I felt something hot strike my back and heard the deafening sound of gunfire. The second shot caused my body to twist around at the impact of the bullet, knocking me to my back on the bed. I was so focus on getting to Shaunie and seeing to her that I pushed aside every protocol and let my guard down. One second of not being on high alert for a threat left me and my girl vulnerable. My mind didn't comprehend that I was shot and down, but my body did, because I couldn't get up no matter how hard I tried. I knew I should be in pain, but the adrenaline surging through me wouldn't allow me to give up the fight. My girl still wasn't safe.

"Noooooooo!" Shaunie screamed. King aimed the gun at Shaunie and pulled the trigger, but it clicked, signaling an empty chamber. I'd never been more relieved in my life! I felt her fumble between us. When she raised her arm, I realized she was reaching for my gun. "Take a head shot. Stay steady," I instructed her in a barely audible whisper. I watched as she raised my 9mm and squeezed the trigger. The bullet flew straight and true, hitting King in his forehead and came out the back of his head. His eyes rolled in and up, and his body jerked back before he fell to his knees. Then he landed face first on the floor. A crimson sea pooled from his head. I watched all this from afar. I felt myself weakening. Slowly, I was losing consciousness from loss of blood. Trying not to succumb to the haze of pain, I attempted to move my arm to grab Shaunie's hand to let her know I was proud of her, but my body felt heavy.

Warm blood ran down my back as I lay helplessly on the bed. "Shaunie." She turned to me with wide eyes as she looked away from the carnage. I knew she was fucked up about catching her first body, but we had to deal with that later.

"Baaaby." She scooted closer to me. Her eyes roved up and down my prone body. "Please don't leave me," she cried. She placed her hand on my face. "I have to stop the blood." She removed her hand from my face and I missed the warmth. Looking behind her, without turning her body, she looked for something. Not once did she put the gun down.

"Help me up." I knew it was dangerous to move me. The bullets went in my back and they didn't exit. This place wasn't secure and any one of King's people could run up on us.

She lifted my torso, but gently laid me back down when the blood leaked like a faucet from my back. In my weakened state, there was no way she would be able to get me to the car without help.

"Get my phone out my pocket and call Thugga n'em." My eyelids felt heavy and I closed my eyes to rest for a second. Now that the immediate danger had passed, I was very aware of the pain.

Digging in my pocket, she placed the phone on the bed and dialed Thugga. At the same time, footsteps pounded through the house. The loud steps made me snap my eyes open.

Quickly focusing on the doorway, Shaunie raised the gun and placed her finger on the trigger, prepared to defend us. I thought I couldn't love her more than I already did, but seeing her take a life to protect us, and continue to defend us, let me know that nothing would ever come between us again.

"Fuck!" Rayne exclaimed as he, Thugga, Killer, and Hassan stood just outside the room. They took in the scene before them that surrounded us. I turned to Shaunie. She had the gun in her blood-covered hand and it was aimed at them. They didn't dare move.

"Bae, it's okay. Lower the gun and let them in." I didn't know if she heard me or not because she didn't put the gun down. I knew the shock of everything that she had just been through controlled her actions. "I need to get to the hospital." She snapped out of her killing daze real quick at the reminder that I was seriously injured. Grabbing my hand, she put the gun down.

My crew rushed into the room and over to the bed. "We got you, my nigga," Thugga said. There was a sense of urgency in his voice. "Rayne, come help me lift him and carry him to the car. Killer and Hassan, take care of this house." He quickly took over as second-in-command.

Thugga placed his hands under my back and lifted me. "Uuurrrggghhh. Fuck!" Pain exploded like firecrackers. It was excruciating and I swear I saw stars. Shaunie squeezed my hand at my outburst due to the intolerable pain. They lifted me fully and carried me through the house.

Every step jostled me and ignited the pain that was running rampant through my body. My chest was already sore from getting shot while wearing my bulletproof vest the night before.

With cans of gasoline in their hands, Killer and Hassan passed us on the way out. Shaunie's eyes looked down at the cans, her mouth pulled into a straight line, and she turned her head for a split second and stared at the cans. With realization of what was going to take place, her eyes sought mine. She didn't ask me to confirm it and I didn't volunteer the information. I knew she didn't approve of how we were going to handle it, but I was glad that her loyalty to me stopped her from voicing it.

When we got to Thugga's car, Shaunie released my hand. She opened the door before she stepped aside and jogged around to the other side of the car, then climbed inside. They put me in the car, placing my head in my girl's lap.

Shaunie stroked my face. "It's going to be okay, baby," she said as she choked back a sob.

I wanted to reassure her that everything was going to be alright, but instead of words, an anguished groan slipped from my lips when Thugga hit a pothole.

"Uuurrrrggghhh," I moaned as we made the journey to the nearest hospital. My insides felt like it was on fire. Black spots danced before my eyes. I tried to stay awake, but the heaviness of my lids was too much for me to hold open. The pain became unbearable. Finally, I succumbed to a pit of darkness.

***

The steady beep of a machine woke me up. My eyes felt heavy and pain traveled up and down my throat when I attempted to swallow. I looked around and it took me a minute to realize I was in a hospital room. To the right, Shaunie was asleep in a reclining chair. To the left, the curtains were drawn, but sunlight peeped through the slit. Using my arms, I struggled to sit up in the hospital bed. I must have made a sound because Shaunie's head popped up off the arm of the chair, her eyes opened and locked on me.

"Thank God you are awake! I was scared to death," she said as she came quickly to the bed. She pushed a button to position the bed to allow my head and torso to sit up. After she fluffed up my pillows, she adjusted the bedding and tucked the covers under me. "I'm so glad that you are going to be fine." She leaned over and placed a kiss to my dry lips.

"Where is everybody?" I needed to be sure my niggas handled everything. I tried to sit up, but my body felt sluggish. Surprisingly, I felt no pain, only a tightness in my back. I looked down at my arm and knew the cause of me not feeling pain was due to whatever meds was flowing through my IV.

"Your mom just left and the guys said they had to handle some things. It's been three days, bae. Everyone has visited every day for hours."

I was thrown back when she said I had been out for three days. My body lost a lot of blood, so I shouldn't have been surprised. "What did the doctor say?"

Ignoring my question, she pushed the call button for the nurse. The nurse's voice boomed over the intercom.

"Yes. What can I help you with?"

"Please let the doctor on call and the nurse assigned to this room know that Keyon Jones just woke up."

"Someone will be down in a minute," the nurse responded.

"Thank You."

Shaunie fidgeted with the covers. That gesture made me nervous. I had been with this woman for so long and I knew her like I knew the back of my hand. She was keeping something from me. "What is it? What did the doctor say?"

She averted her eyes from me. "They will be in any minute to check on you and tell you what's going on." She didn't give me an answer and my patience was running thin.

"I ain't gon' ask you again. What did..." My words trailed off as the door opened.

The doctor walked into the room, along with a nurse. I studied his face, noticing the crease in his forehead as he read my chart. Not being able to decipher that look, I focused on the nurse as she pulled her cart beside her.

"I need to check your vitals, Mr. Jones," the nurse said.

I nodded my head as the nurse placed the blood pressure cuff on my arm and the thermometer in my mouth. She checked the reading on the machine and wrote the numbers down on a chart. My eyes drifted to Shaunie who stood aside as the nurse worked and the doctor waited patiently at the foot of the bed. She seemed hesitant to maintain eye contact as she fidgeted with the blanket.

When the nurse was done and left the room, the doctor stepped forward.

"I'm Dr. Daliet, the attending physician. Mr. Jones, I am going to do a quick examination and then we will talk about the procedure we did when you came in with gunshot wounds."

"Cool."

The doctor checked my arms and hands. He asked me to squeeze. After I squeezed his hand, he proceeded to my legs, starting with my feet, to check the plantar reflexes. Starting at the heel and stopping at my toes, he took a silver pointed object and scraped the bottom of my feet. My heart started pounding double time when I didn't feel the sensation. The external stimuli should have produced an uncontrollable urge to jerk or move in conscious patients.

The doctor looked up. "Did you feel that?"

I looked away from my legs to look at him. "No." I looked back at my legs and willed them to move, but they refused. Shaunie came to my side and grabbed my hand in hers. I looked up at her and she had a small, strained smile on her face. Tears filled her eyes, but didn't fall.

"Let's try something else." Dr. Daliet took a plexor from his coat pocket. He lightly tapped the patellar tendon, just below the kneecap. Getting no response, he tried the other knee.

The whole time he examined me, I stared at my legs, willing them to move as if I had super powers. Panic, pure and simple, pierced through me. *Move!* I willed my legs, but they refused to obey my command. Shaunie's hand tightened on mine, but I ignored it. My heart was racing and my breathing pattern changed to pants. I leaned back against the pillow with my eyes closed tight. Trying to suppress the tears of frustration, my mind became a world of recrimination as I mentally raged at the world and myself for being in this situation.

"Mr. Jones, you were shot in the back three times. One bullet hit…"

He droned on and on about the accident and surgical procedure, but all I heard was "incomplete spinal cord injury and paralysis." Everything else faded to the background as his voice died away. I became lost in my rage of being rendered helpless and my sadness that my girl was stuck with half of a man.

Chapter 6

Loyalty is unwavering in good times and bad.

-Proverbs 17:17

Shaunie

Holding the plate of food in my hand, I walked into the room heading toward the bed. It hurt my heart every time I saw Keyz. He looked so despondent and dejected sitting in the bed staring at the TV, without really watching it. There was a tired hopelessness etched in his face. No amount of cajoling seemed to be able to help his mood. Keira's soft words, kisses, and hugs didn't work either. It's been two weeks since Keyz had been discharged from the rehabilitation center. After we were informed that Keyz had a slim chance of walking again, he was transferred to an inpatient facility. However, his time there didn't last long, because he refused to do anything there and signed himself out after ranting and raving.

After being released from the facility, his mom and I decided it would be best if we moved into her house. It was going to be too hard for me to care for him and Keira. We could have hired a live-in nurse, but Keyz was a proud man and I knew he wouldn't want anyone being around him, especially a stranger, while he was vulnerable. I didn't mind taking care of him. My love and loyalty was unwavering.

"Hey, bae. I brought your lunch." I placed the plate on the tray and rolled it closer to the bed. When he didn't reply, I tried again. "You have to eat something." I walked to the bed and placed a kiss to his forehead while running my fingers through his dreads. His dreads needed to be done, but he refused to let me do it. I couldn't imagine what he was going through, but I tried every day to show him and let him know I was there for him. Frustration was slowly

beginning to get to me because of Keyz' attitude and difficult behavior, but I constantly strived to stay calm.

"Keira asked about you today. She really wants to see her daddy.
How about we get you cleaned up and let her visit?" He stared, unblinking, straight ahead. "Keyz, you have to eat and get cleaned,
now." I rolled the tray over his bed.

Before I could step back, he knocked the tray over and pulled
himself up by the arms. "I don't want to fucking eat and I don't want
your fucking ass in here with me."

Closing my eyes and counting to three, I tried to remind myself
what he was going through. Hell, what we were going through.
While he was laid up in bed and wore physical scars, I carried mental
scars. I watched a man whom I had been intimate with get killed,
the love of my life was shot, and I took a life. The first few nights
after the kidnapping, I was plagued with nightmares of reliving the
moment of getting kidnapped and pulling the trigger, ending Dam's
brother's life. But after a seeing Keyz struggle to pull through, those
nightmares and feelings were pushed away. They were misplaced
feelings. Dam's brother explicitly told me what he was going to do
to me and what he would have done to my daughter. I took comfort
in the fact that I protected mine at all cost. Opening my eyes, I focused on him. This was the first reaction I got from him, so I guess
this reaction was better than no reaction. "Listen," I began.

"No, you listen. Why the fuck are you still here? You want to be
stuck with a fucking cripple, changing my piss bag and shit. Go.
Leave! You will eventually." He screamed.

The commotion was heard through the house. I heard Keira crying and Ms. Lynn's footsteps headed our way.

"I'm not going no gotdamn where. Where in the fuck did you
get that from?" I walked back to the bed and grabbed his face. I
wanted to cry at his pain and mine, but I had to be strong for the both
of us.

He jerked his head away, trying to get out of my grasp, but I refused to let go until he heard me. "Move, Shaunie."

I grabbed him in a firm grip. "No. I'm not leaving you. I love you. The doctor said it was a possibility you would never walk again. That's not written in stone. We can get you physical therapy and try. We have to try." He needed to snap out of the self-pity and put some effort into getting healthy and well, even if he doesn't walk again.

He dipped his eyes away from me, but I persisted. I was fighting for my family.

"Now, I am going to go to the kitchen and make you some more food. I expect you to eat it and then I am going to bathe you. No more problems, Keyz. We have to get through this for Keira," I paused, "and Shaun. They need you. I need you."

I backed away from the bed. When I turned around, Ms. Lynn was standing in the doorway with a smile on her face and Keira on her hip. As I passed by her, she nodded her head in approval of me standing firm with Keyz. I had to show tough love to make my family whole again. I knew what he was going through was difficult, but sulking wasn't going to change anything.

Ms. Lynn followed me into the kitchen. I grabbed a plate from the cabinet and started fixing a plate to take back to Keyz' room for his lunch. She placed Keira on the counter next to me and she stood before her to catch her if she fell.

"You did right back there. He got to move on."

"I know. I don't want to be mean to him, but he has to keep moving forward. He has a family to live for." I leaned over and placed a kiss to my baby's cheek. She often fussed and whined because she couldn't climb over her daddy and her daddy couldn't get up and play with her like she was used to.

Ms. Lynn grabbed my hand as I reached into a pot, forcing me to look at her. "Thank you for being here with him. Many other women would have left at the first sign of trouble. I'm glad he has you to love him, unconditionally. It takes a strong woman to stand with her man when faced with the challenges y'all are facing. I love you like a daughter. Thank you for loving my baby," she said, ending the last bit on a choked sob.

I placed the plate on the counter. Pulling her into a hug, I held her tight. I have never seen her cry. She always seemed so strong and infallible. Tears falling from my eyes, we took comfort from each other.

Keira got impatient at being left out. She tugged my hair. "Hug too, mommy." She held her arms out for me to get her. Ms. Lynn and I chuckled lightly.

Lifting her up, I placed her on my hip. "Okay, mommy's baby. Hug for you, too." We hugged again with Keira in the middle.

After a few minutes, Ms. Lynn stepped back. She wiped her eyes with her hands, then moved to the counter to grab a dish towel and began wiping down the counter as awkward silence fell over us, but the silence wasn't uncomfortable. It was interrupted by nothing but the noise Keira made as she played with her play kitchen set in the corner. Just like her son, her pride ran a mile long and she was embarrassed to show weakness. I turned around and continued to fix Keyz' food.

"I'm going to bring this to Keyz. Can you watch Keira?"

She waved me away as she continued to wipe down the kitchen counters, as she struggled to get her emotions under control.

When I walked inside the bedroom, Keyz turned toward me. I was shocked because he usually ignored everyone. I hoped our talk helped, because I was tired. Pulling the emotional weight for everybody and the physical stress was taking a toll on me.

"Are you ready to eat?" I placed the food on the tray and stepped back. I didn't want to crowd him. He needed to feel capable and like a man if he had any chance of getting back in the right frame of mind.

50

"Yeah." He moved the tray closer, picked up his fork, and dug in.

Busying myself with cleaning up the mess on the floor, I hid a smile. The battle was won, but we still had a war. Physical therapy was next on the agenda. When I was done cleaning, I sat in the chair next to the bed. Keyz continued to eat.

Placing my head in my hand that was on the arm rest, I closed my eyes for a second while my love finally ate without an argument. My head jerking back woke me up from my stolen cat nap. I looked to the bed and Key was staring at me. Our eyes locked. I couldn't help but see the turbulent emotions that he contained within himself.

"Come here," he told me.

At his beckon, my feet moved before my sluggish mind registered his command. I walked to the bed and stopped before him. He twisted his torso so he was facing me. "What is it, bae?"

He patted the bed on the other side of him. As a safety precaution, we purchased a bed with rails and he was able to recline up and down for his comfort. I climbed in the bed and he opened his arms for me. Being careful of everything that he was hooked up to, I snuggled close and rested my head on his strong chest. This was the first time he even attempted to touch me, let alone hold me. I didn't realize how much I had missed those simple touches from him. He was my everything, apart from Keira. Even though he felt he wasn't whole, he was still the same to me.

Familiar hands ran through the strands of my hair. The act was so soothing. It was like a balm to my soul and tattered emotions. I inhaled deeply, taking in his scent. I could stay in his arms until the end of time.

Breaking the silence, he spoke first. "I'm sorry for how I acted earlier and how I treated you. This is hard for me. I can't stand the thought of never walking again. It makes me feel less of a man. I don't feel like a man. I can't even pick up my daughter like I use to or play ball with Shaun anymore. This hurts."

A tear fell down his face. His words caused my heart to constrict in my chest. This was so hard for such a proud man. Wiping the tear away, I sat up and grabbed his face. "Everything has changed, I know. You may not be able to play with the kids like before, but you can still play with them and be here for them."

I still held his face in my hands, but his eyes shifted away. "What about you?"

"What about me?" My brows creased in confusion.

"I can't get a hard on to please you anymore." The crux of most of the problems was revealed in that one sentence. Sex always played a big part in our relationship. We were very active and hardly went a day without sex.

"Baby. I love you. We can't fully have sex, but nothing is wrong with your tongue," I said to lighten the mood.

He tickled my side and I laughed.

"Seriously. We just have to find creative ways. Plus, the doctor said there was a chance that you wouldn't walk again. His answer wasn't definite. With physical therapy and time, anything could happen." Optimism was my new best friend. We had so much bad to happen to us in such a short period of time, the only thing left was something good.

"I hope so, bae. Imma try to be positive, but you gotta respect my mood when I get in my mental. Not being able to walk is a hard pill to swallow for anybody. I'm bound to have some bad days."

I pulled a dread. "As long as those bad days don't involve you throwing food. Your ass is going to pick it up the next time. But good or bad days, we get through them together, okay." I waited for his answer.

"Together." He pushed my head back down to his chest and continued to run his fingers through my hair until I fell asleep in his arms.

Chapter 7

People who are loyal to you through your darkest hours, are the only ones who deserve to be with you during your brightest hours.
-Unknown

Keyz

I threw the file down on the table and looked back at Shaunie with a scowl on my face. "I don't like any of them," I told her without pause. Papers and files were strewn all over the table. We were looking over resumes of the applicants who applied for the physical therapy position. After hours of pouring over documents and referrals, we were both exhausted.

Rolling her eyes, Shaunie picked up the files and placed them in a stack. "Well, I like Ramon Torres. He has a very impressive resume and there is no doubt of his credentials." She leaned on the desk, standing next to my wheelchair. The wheelchair was delivered three days ago. I thought I would hate being in the chair like an invalid, but it provided me with mobility and that was better than being laid up in the bed all day. Every day was getting better and better. My upper body strength helped me to move around. Whenever I got too tired or too weak, my girl or my mom was there to assist me. My crew came by several times over the past few weeks, but I wasn't ready to face them. Mentally, my state of mind was fragile and physically, I was vulnerable. They proved their loyalty to me and I didn't question it. However, with the Qwan situation and all, doubts lingered.

This Ramon character was a Spanish pretty boy and I didn't want him around me or my girl. "Well, I like Ms. Woods." I didn't really like the plastic-looking bitch. Everything about her screamed trouble. Her sensuality didn't fit her job or her credentials. No matter what accolades she received, I knew Shaunie wasn't with her hanging around for no type of job. I wasn't with it either. My relationship was on solid ground and I didn't need nothing or no one to shake it up. We seemed to reach an understanding after the talk we had last week. The easy banter and comfortability we always enjoyed between us was back like there was never any problems.

"Ms. Woods like wood and she ain't getting shit this way. No sir. Next," she said, shutting that down real quick. A trace of a smile played on my lips at her comment.

Reaching over quickly, I grabbed her and pulled her on my lap. She landed on me with a girlish squeal. Today was a good day and the smile on her face told me so. Everything wasn't gravy all the time. I still had bad days when the depression of living handicapped got me down. It took me a minute to get used to not feeling sensations when she or Keira was on my lap or touching my legs. "What you worried about? I can't get my wood up."

"Don't say that!" She struggled on my lap. I knew she hated when I said stuff about me being paralyzed.

"Bae, chill. It's the truth. I can't fuck her. I don't even want to. My eyes are on you." I kissed her lips.

"I love you so much, Keyz." She returned the kiss. Our kiss deepened. I didn't feel anything, not even a twitch, in my lower region, but Shaunie was quickly becoming aroused from our kiss. Her breath came in short pants and little moans escaped her throat.

My hands wrapped in her silky hair as our tongues curled sensually together. Breaking the kiss, I moved my head away. "Take your clothes off and lay on the desk." We hadn't been intimate, in any capacity, since before I got shot. My girl was horny and I wanted to see to her needs, even though I wouldn't be able to get pleasure myself from the full act. I would enjoy eating her pussy.

She hesitated before she did what I said. The cool air against her bare flesh hardened her nipples, making them erect. When she lay back on the office desk, I grabbed her legs and pulled her to the edge.

Placing her legs on my shoulders, I leaned forward and placed soft kisses on her inner thigh as my warm hands traveled up her stomach to her breast. Her stomach quivered when my fingers skimmed along her skin. Reaching my destination, my thumb caressed her nipples.

"Baby, that feels so good." She thrust her full breast into my hands. I pulled back my right hand and spread her legs apart. My fingers slowly ran up and down her folds, parting them to access her sensitive clit. Her juices trickled from her body. Slowly, I pushed my finger into her slippery wet core. Her heat engulfed me.

In and out my fingers moved. She matched the paced and rhythm of my fingers as I finger fucked her. While my fingers worked, my thumb rubbed and applied pressure to her clit. When she tightened her muscles, I pulled my hand free from between her legs. Not giving her a chance to move, I bent my head forward. Licking my lips, moistening them, I was ready to taste her. I swiped my tongue. The taste of her was sweet. Shaunie arched her back, bringing her pussy fully in my face, giving my tongue full access. "Damn, bae, this pussy taste so good." Her fingers brushed my dreads as I gave her pleasure.

Her moans made me go ham on her pussy with my tongue. I surged my tongue inside of her. Sucking and slurping sounds filled the office.

"Yes, just like that," she moaned, with her eyes half-closed. She grabbed my head and ground herself on my tongue. I ate her out like I was a starving man. Her legs started to jerk and I knew she was close. Sticking my finger back into her, I kept my tongue on her clit.

She shattered, screaming my name, short nails digging into my scalp as she came. I lapped every drop of her flowing juices. When she finished her climax and her trembling subsided, I moved my kisses to her stomach. Laying my head there, I felt contentment. I wasn't able to be inside her, but I still pleased her. After everything I put her through, she was still here, with me. Moments like this, being with her, was worth more than any material thing or money I have.

Suddenly, the door burst open, causing us both to jump and look in that direction. "What the fuck?" I said as I looked at the intruders.

"Aaaahhhh!" Shaunie let out a bloodcurdling scream when she realized they got a full view of her nudity. Faster than the eyes could see, she dodged behind the desk, out of their line of vision.

Thugga, Killer, and Rayne stood frozen in shock in the doorway. Quickly recovering, Thugga coughed and averted his eyes. "My bad, we gon' wait in the front room," he muttered, grabbing the door, closing it behind them. I heard laughter from the hall and knew they thought the shit was funny.

I looked at Shaunie, her head was peeking from behind the desk looking at the door. Her cheeks were flaming red from being caught naked. "Come on, bae, let's go see what these fools want."

She shook her head. "Hell no. They just saw me in all my naked glory, spread out like a buffet with my kitty in your face and you want me to go see them. Hell no! You go see them." She stood up and began to put her clothes back on.

I knew she was embarrassed that they saw her naked. When we first got together, it took her a long time to be comfortable with me before she bared it all. "Imma go see what's up then. Come give me a kiss." She bent over and kissed me quickly on the lips.

"I'm going to go hide out in the room until they leave." When she walked passed me to get to the door, I slapped her on the ass.

Turning around, her beautiful hazel eyes glared at me. "That shit hurts, Keyz, with your heavy-handed ass.

"You know you like that." I reached down to the push rim of the wheelchair. Giving it a push, I lunged forward, continuing the motion until I made it through the door. Shaunie went to the bedroom and I proceeded to the living room where my niggas waited.

The wheels of the wheelchair barely made a sound on the hardwood floor. I pushed along the hall that opened up to the living room. Killer and Rayne sat on the sofa watching TV. They watched me as I entered, but they didn't say anything. Thugga came from the direction of the kitchen with a sandwich in his hand. "What's up, my niggas?" I asked them.

"Nothing man, just coming to holla at you and run down some business."

Taking a bite of his sandwich, Thugga said, "Man, you got something on your lip." He pointed to me.

I reached up to my face, but I felt nothing. Killer and Rayne began to chuckle.

"Nigga, you ain't brush your teeth before you came to talk to us. This nigga got pussy breathe and he want talk," Thugga said.

Just that fast, it was like everything that went down the past few days disappeared. Laughing with my dawgs reminded me of all the shit we went through, but always made it together. "Nigga fuck you."

I rolled my chair in front of the sofa and Thugga took a seat on the love seat across from the sofa. First things first, business.

Thugga took over as second-in-command since I been down. Profits were coming in at an all-time high. King was eliminated so whoever was dealing with him and his few crew members were copping from us on the corners and with bigger orders of product. No trap houses had been hit by 504 or robberies. Rayne met with Alejandro to arrange shipment since he was already handling shipments on our end. Killer set up two more traps. One in New Orleans East and another on the Westbank in Marrero. My crew was able to handle business and keep the team running in my absence.

"Good looking. Y'all seem like everything is in control, I appreciate y'all keeping everything running smoothly."

"We *fam!* This want we do," Killer said.

"*Fam!*" We all said simultaneously.

Not wanting to break up our moment of basking in loyalty to the team, I was reluctant to bring up Qwan's betrayal, but it needed to be discussed. "Now, what we got with the whole Qwan situation?"

The room got quiet and the temperature dropped several degrees. Everybody was in their feelings over his betrayal. It was hard to comprehend how someone so close to a person could do that person harm, but shit like that happened every day, in the hood and in the suburbs.

Rayne blew out a breath. He leaned over, placing his elbows on his knees, fingers linked together, facing me. "The shit is unreal. The burner phone revealed two of the soldiers working with him. We picked them up and got some info outta them. They sold the product that Qwan was stealing when he robbed the trap houses, but they wasn't behind any shootings."

"I trust they were dealt with," I stated.

"What's left of them is in the swamp, but I'm sure the gators got to them already," Killer said.

"Cool." Rayne looked at Thugga. Killer shifted in his seat.

I looked at each of them, waiting for someone to spit it out, whatever it was that was on their mind. "Niggas, what?"

"NeNe hoe ass number was in Qwan's burner phone. There were text messages between them. It was a setup all along with that bitch. A whole fucking year!" Thugga exclaimed. "The snake ass nigga and bitch plotted and schemed on you. On us."

I was surprised that hoe was knee deep in the bullshit. She purposely exposed me fucking her to Shaunie. That right there should have told me the bitch was on to something. No other chick stepped out of line, everybody else played their position.

Karma was a bitch though. There I was fucking over a good woman for a bitch that would just as soon cut my throat. I blamed myself for being in the situation I was in. My focus should have been on my family and running my empire instead of allowing myself to get distracted by fast women with easy pussy. "Fuck that bitch and fuck Qwan."

"That shit is fucking crazy yo. That nigga been part of the crew since day one," Killer rubbed his hand over his low fade.

I remember all of us, as lil' niggas, running the streets. We had plans to make some real money. Eventually that dream became a reality. We all were eating good. But like any other crew, someone fell victim to greed and envy, no matter how noble their ambitions were at the beginning. Fortunately for me, his greed made him blind and he made mistakes and was caught in the nick of time.

"It's fucked up, but we gotta keep it moving. The threat was eliminated. Time to get back to making money." It is what it is. I didn't want to look back. Moving forward was my only goal.

Nikki Tee

Chapter 8

One loyal girlfriend is worth a hundred hoes.

-Unknown

Shaunie

At the sound of the front door opening, I jumped up from my position on the sofa in the living room. Nervous energy coursed through me. Tucking my hair behind my ear, I faced the door. My palms were sweaty, so I wiped them down on my skirt.

Keyz looked up from playing with Keira, who was sitting on his lap. "It's okay, bae, it ain't like he doesn't know you."

I wanted to make a good impression and hoped he would be comfortable around me. This was the first time Shaun was visiting since Keyz got shot. It was also the first time he and I would have spent any time together since I got fired from being his teacher. He had been to his grandma's house numerous times before, but this was the first time I would be here while he stayed the weekend. Keyz and I were back together so that meant Shaun was going to be a permanent fixture in not just their lives but mine.

"I know. I know."

Shaun and Ms. Lynn walked into the room. Ms. Lynn volunteered to pick him up for us since Keyz wasn't able and I wasn't ready to deal with Ashley on no level. I was trying to accept Shaun, but that didn't mean I had to have any dealings with his mother. She had caused enough trouble and to date, no encounter we've ever had has been amicable. It was best to keep Shaun as far away from that kind of drama as possible.

"Hey Daddy," Shaun said when he walked fully into the room.

When Keira heard her brother's voice, her head popped up from the toy she played with. "Shaun," she squealed with excitement. She climbed off her dad and ran to her brother as fast as her little legs could. He picked her up when she reached him and kissed her cheek. Seeing my daughter's reaction to her brother and seeing their interaction told me that I had made the right decision by putting aside my feelings and allowing them to have a relationship.

Ms. Lynn sat on the loveseat with a smile on her face.

"What's up, lil' man? Come over here and give me some dap." Shaun put Keira down and walked over to his dad. Keyz held out his fist for a pound.

Hesitantly, Shaun approached his dad who was sitting in his wheelchair next to the sofa. As I watched his face, I knew he had a million questions about his dad being in the chair.

"Hey, daddy." He gave his dad some dap and stood before him, seemingly unsure what to do.

Keyz patted his lap. "Come sit here."

He climbed on his lap. His movements were slow. I realized he thought he would hurt him. Shaun always was a good kid. Even in school he was thoughtful and helped the other kids.

My daughter ran to me when she saw her position on her daddy's lap was filled. Putting her hands out to be picked up, I lifted her and put her on my hip. I stood there and watched the guys in my life have a little reunion.

"We gotta get you a haircut, buddy. I see your mama let it grow out too much. Imma have your uncle Thugga come and take you to go get one when he takes Lil' Thugga to the barber."

I noticed his appearance when he first walked in the door, but didn't comment on it. He was in bad need of a haircut and his clothes looked dirty. Ashley usually made sure he had clean clothes and I found out Keyz kept him with a fresh cut. It had only been a few weeks since the shooting, so I didn't understand how his upkeep could decline, knowing for a fact Keyz made sure Ashley received money for him.

"Okay, daddy. What happened to make you in a wheelchair?" he asked his dad with his head down, staring at his shoes. He seemed so unsure about things. Shaun used to be so inquisitive and he used to smile all the time. My heart went out to him. First, his father kept him at a distance because he didn't want me to find out about him. Then he gets a new teacher mid-year after his mom came to my job acting a fool. Now, his father was in a wheelchair and he struggled to understand why. At a time when he should be enjoying his childhood and being carefree, the decisions the adults around him made were slowly withering away his childhood.

Keyz' eyes searched me out and I gave him an encouraging smile. We anticipated him asking. Knowing we had to delicately handle the way we told Shaun of the accident, we rehearsed what to say so that he would be able to understand.

"I was in an accident and hurt my legs. They are very weak right now and I can't walk. I have to exercise to make them strong again."

"Does it hurt?" he asked, looking Keyz in the eyes.

"No, son. It doesn't."

"Can you still play football with me?" Shaun's voice was full of hope. Football was one of the few things him and his father did together.

Keyz' throat convulsed. I knew the question was painful. It was one of the reasons he was so depressed after the accident. The thought of not being able to play with his kids the way he used to was too much to handle. "I can still catch and throw the ball to you. I just can't run."

Shaun nodded his head. "That's cool. I can still play football with Lil' Thugga and play tag with Keira."

A smile lit up Keyz' face at the easy acceptance from his son. "I love you, lil' man. Now, go say hello to Shaunie."

The corners on my lips automatically pulled into a smile when he faced me. "Hey Shaun." I hefted my baby higher on my hip. I wanted to reach out and pulled him to me, but was afraid to do so. Worry tugged at me that his mom may have said things in front of him to turn him away from me. Fear of rejection held me back. Not once did I realize he may be feeling exactly like me.

"Hey, Ms. Shaunie." He looked down at the floor. At the silence, I looked at Keyz, but he just looked back at me.

"I'm glad you are here with us. Keira has being asking for you." He looked at me with a small smile on his face. I couldn't help but to worry what he had been told about me. He was never this reserved toward me.

"I have a surprise for you." I put Keira down and she ran right to her favorite man. Picking up Shaun's bag by the door, I turned. "Follow me."

He followed me down the hall. When we got to the last door on the left, I turned the knob, pushed opened the door and stepped back so he could walk into the room.

"An Avengers bedroom? How cool!" He ran into the room. Taking everything in, he couldn't stay in one spot as he touched the bed then went to the toy chest. Excitement was evident in the way he took out each toy and examined them.

Our residence was temporarily located at Ms. Lynn's house. Wanting Shaun to feel like he was at home and not just visiting, I asked Keyz about his favorite characters. His room was decked out with the Avengers theme.

"I'm so glad you like it, Shaun." Following him inside his bedroom with his bag in my hand, I walked over to the chest to put away his clothes. An unnerving smell wafted from the bag as I partially opened it. When it was fully opened, a rancid odor of dampness hung from the clothes inside. It was so bad it was making me sick.

I gagged from the smell. My nose scrunched up and I discreetly turned my head away. It was so overwhelming, I quickly zipped the bag up. His clothes needed serious washing. *Why would that bitch, Ashley, send that child here with wet clothes that stink?*

Picking up the bag, I turned to walk away. "You stay in here and play with your new toys. Me and your dad will be back in in a few," I said looking over my shoulder at him.

"Okay," he said as he pulled out his Legos.

I walked back into the living room to find Keyz, Keira, and Ms. Lynn watching Despicable Me. They didn't follow me and Shaun in the room, because they wanted to give us a few minutes to bond without them.

Keyz noticed me first. My facial expression must have indicated that something was wrong. When he opened his mouth to ask me what was wrong, I looked at Keira and shook my head. I didn't want to discuss anything in front of her. She may be young, but she was smart and listened. A lot of parents made the mistake of talking about things in front of their kids that they shouldn't. They needed to realize that kids repeat whatever they hear.

"Keira," Keyz said when he looked at me. "Go play with Shaun." Without a word, she got up and ran to her brother's room.

Not wanting to overstep any boundaries, I took a deep breath and tried to find the right words to express my concern. I didn't want to seem like I was looking for something to have against Ashley, but I didn't appreciate her sending her child, *my man's child*, with wet clothes. Surely, he had more than just these few outfits. I couldn't understand how a woman could mistreat her own child just to get back at the other parent. Didn't she realize that it only reflected poorly on her and not the child?

Why the fuck am I worrying about stepping over boundaries? I thought. Saying fuck it, I spoke my mind. I held up the bag. "Shaun's clothes are wet and they smell. A lot of baby mama's do stupid shit like sending dirty clothes or no clothes at all. You need to call her and check her ass. We ain't starting with the shenanigans. We are going to start this the way we plan to finish this. I don't appreciate it not one bit."

That wasn't what I planned to say, but what the hell. Keyz ass better understand where I was coming from or we were going to have a problem.

"When I picked up Shaun, that thot looked like she was headed to the street corner. Her ass cheeks was hanging out her shorts. She rushed Shaun out the house like he was a disease she wanted to get rid of. I didn't say shit to her, because I don't like her." Ms. Lynn ended her little rant with a smack of her teeth.

"She slipping for real. I wanted to call her ass and cuss her out when I saw him hit the door. My lil' man's hair looking all nappy and shit. I peeped out how dirty the clothes were that he's wearing. I thought maybe he had been outside playing or something."

Men and their stupidity. That type of dirt wasn't grass stains. The spots on his clothes looked stained with crusted-over food and other unidentifiable things.

"Take care of it now." I turned and walked away to go to the laundry room, but Ms. Lynn grabbed the bag.

"I got it. I'll throw them in the washer then go run to the store and grab him a few things."

"Thanks," I said as she walked out the room leaving me and Keyz alone. I didn't think to buy him extra clothes and things to keep here. Thinking we were all adults, I thought she would handle it like a woman and send her child with the proper things he needed for a weekend stay. I tried to give her the benefit of the doubt without the feelings I had for her clouding my mind.

When I turned to leave back out the room to go play with the kids, Keyz called out to me.

"Bae..."

"Yeah?" I lifted my eyebrow as I waited for him to speak. He knew I was a little peeved by Ashley's antics. I never heard about her doing this in the past when he visited, so I knew she did it because she knew I was back with Keyz and likely was going to be here.

"Imma get at her and get her straight."

I nodded and turned away. I was trusting him to do what was right for our family. Shaun was now part of our family. He had better get his baby mama in order or I will.

***

A sigh of relaxation escaped my lips when I finally laid down on the bed next to Keyz. It had been a long weekend. Between two extremely active kids and taking care of Keyz, I was exhausted. Not long after his arrival, Shaun relaxed and fit right in around me like he had when I was his teacher. I didn't realize how much I missed his little personality. When Keira fell down while running outside, Shaun quickly stopped playing and ran over to her before I could. As me, Keyz, and Ms. Lynn watched him check her grass stained knee then dusted her off, I wanted to cry. He made me think of my son that I aborted and how he would have been an amazing protector to his little sister. I was glad that Shaun stepped in and will be that protector.

I laid my head on Keyz' chest. The steady rhythm of his heartbeat further relaxed me. As he gently stroked my hair, another sigh fell from my mouth.

Brushing his lips against the top of my head, he whispered, "What are you thinking?"

"Our little family is exhausting. I'm out of practice. When I was teaching, I used to be able to keep up with twenty five year olds. Now, I just want to fall asleep," I told him, keeping my head right where it belonged, on my name that was tatted on his chest over his heart.

He tugged my hair, forcing me to look up at him. "Thank you. Thank you for taking me back and caring for me. I love you so much. I am so sorry for all the hurt and pain that I caused you. Just know that my love for you will never go away. I'll gladly die for you. Thank you for accepting my son, even though you didn't have to make him feel a part of our family. I know it isn't easy when he is a constant reminder of my infidelity."

I placed my hand on his cheek and he nuzzled it. "It is a struggle, I'm not going to lie. But I know you love him and I see how much Keira loves him. I loved him before I knew he was yours. We can't truly move on together if your child can't be around you when I'm around. That's not how it works. It's hard, really hard. But all I can do is try."

Rubbing his cheek against my hair, he moved his head to the inside of my neck and kissed it softly. "I got a surprise."

"What is it?"

"Look down at my feet and watch my toes."

I looked down at his toes and waited for what he wanted to show me. It took a few seconds, but what I saw made me gasp. The movement of his toes was almost imperceptible, one wouldn't be able to tell they moved.

Jumping up, I walked to the end of the bed to get a closer look. "Do it again!" When he moved them again, tears formed in my eyes.

"Don't get too excited. Ramon said it's too early to tell anything. He said it could be spasms. I think it's not, because I can move it on command now if I try really hard."

"Baby, you wiggled your toes." I was so happy. Even though he barely moved them, it was a start. The doctor said he didn't know the exact extent of damage, but there was a slim possibility he would regain movement with extensive therapy and exercise. First thing in the morning, I was calling the doctor's office for an appointment for Keyz.

"Now, stop talking and let me show you what else I can wiggle." He stuck his tongue out and flicked it in rapid succession.

Not wanting to disappointment him, I sashayed to him and proceeded to let him show me.

Chapter 9

Blood makes you related, loyalty makes you family.

-Unknown

Keyz

Sweat poured down my body and my arms shook from the strain. Beads of salty moisture trickled down to my nose. My jaws were clinched and my eyes were narrowed as I stared at the spot that was my goal for today. I wanted to stop so badly and rest for a second, but I persevered.

I gripped the bar handle as I took a step. My steps were slow and measured. Every day I pushed myself harder and harder. After the night I showed Shaunie I had a little movement in my toes and my doctor confirmed I may be able to regain some movement, I went into beast mode with my workouts.

"Don't stop. Keep going to the mark. Let's go!" Ramon coached me on with a yell.

That Rico Suave muthafucka was damn good at his job. We mapped out a game plan and followed through. Only three weeks into physical therapy and I had feelings back in my legs. I could move them a little, but not enough for me to walk on them. I basically had to learn to walk again. My nerves and muscles had to be strengthened. I had my reservations about having dude around my girl and family, but after his second interview when he informed us that he was gay, I hired him on the spot. He was batting for the same team as my girl, so I had no worries.

"I got this," I said in between breaths that puffed out through my mouth. Refocusing, I concentrated harder and took another step. Step by step, I made it to the mark. When I did, I sagged with relief. Ramon stepped up and assisted me to the massage table that was set up in the den. It had been cleared out to make space for the equipment I needed.

The distance I walked with the bars today was the farthest I had walked so far. Most of the strain was on my arms, but my legs handled what they could. Inside me, pride was a living, breathing entity. But overriding that feeling was humility. I was deeply humbled and grateful to have the opportunity to be alive. Taking several steps with the assistance of the bar encouraged me to push harder.

"You did real good today. We are going to do the same distance tomorrow, but then the next day you'll rest," he said with a slight accent. "Now, I'm going to rub down your muscles so you don't cramp."

In the beginning of my sessions, it felt unmanly having this nigga help me when I was going to fall or to rub on my legs. But fuck that feeling unmanly shit. I was secure in my manhood. That shit wasn't going to help me to walk so I can play with my kids or to better fuck my girl. As long as he didn't try no funny shit, we was cool.

I laid back as his hands worked the kinks from my sore muscles. Every muscle in my legs ached. The first night after one of our sessions I refused to let that nigga rub me down. I paid the price for it through the night because I had spasms for hours, alternating between legs.

Shaunie had to help me to the bath to soak in warm water to help ease the discomfort. My baby stayed up all night with me, rubbing my legs until the pain subsided. A few hours had passed when I finally settled down enough to get some sleep.

"Keyz." Her voice brought me out of my musing. I turned my head to look at her. She leaned on the door frame with her head peeking in the room.

"What's up, bae?" I motioned her over to me with a hand wave. She walked into the room, stopped in front of me, and placed a quick kiss to my lips.

"You have a visitor."

My eyebrows dipped in confusion. My crew just left this morning and everyone else knew not to bother me while I was back here. "Who?"

"Kamal."

Now I really was confused. I knew who Kamal was, but he wasn't really a close friend of mine. Definitely not close enough to be dropping by unannounced to my mama's house. I only fucked with him on the strength on my dawg, Yuriah. "Help me up and in my chair, Ram," I called him by the nickname I gave him. Ramon coming from my mouth sounded funny as hell. The fucking name sounded feminine. "Bae, send him back here for me."

"Okay, love. You need anything?" Shaunie asked me.

"Nah, I'm straight."

While I waited for Kamal to come back, I wiped the sweat off my face and neck with a towel. Ramon packed up his bag and was getting ready to head out after confirming our standing appointment for tomorrow. Satisfied I was going to follow his care instruction, he walked out the door just as Kamal was coming in.

I took a minute to size him up. His wasn't exactly a friend or a foe. We were about the same size, build and height. My skin tone was darker than his. I wondered, *What the fuck he was doing here?*

Kamal walked over to me and I dapped him up. "So, what brings you here, unannounced?" I asked getting straight to the point.

He sat down in the chair across from me. "Look round, since you want to cut the bullshit and get to the reason for my visit, here it is. Imma Jones."

"What that mean? A lot of people are Joneses."

The look he gave me made me feel like I was missing something. I was tired as hell from my workout and all I wanted to do was shower and sleep, in that order. Solving riddles wasn't on my agenda.

"You think I would come all the way over here to tell you we have the same last name without it meaning shit? Fool, we got the same damn sperm donor."

I didn't care that his tone took on an edge. My head was spinning. All my life I grew up thinking I was my father's only child. The few times I did see him, he never mentioned me having any siblings on his side. Knowing that he left my mom and me, I shouldn't be surprised he left his seeds here and there.

"Man," I scratched my head, not knowing what to say. "That's some foul shit not to say anything to us about it."

"For real. I only found out because I ran across him in the hood and he told me you were shot. Then, he just said go visit your brother and walked off. I had to hem him up to find out what shit he was spitting."

This shit was un-fucking-real. Nigga 'round here living his life not doing shit. What if me and Kamal had some beef and tried to take out each other? My trigger game was crazy and I heard Kamal's was a beast, too. Both of us would have been fucked up about it if we had learned we were brothers after some bullshit had happened.

"What he say?"

He leaned over with his elbows on his knees and sighed. Lines of exhaustion wrinkled his forehead. "Basically, he was messing with your mama and mine at the same time. Both got pregnant and he dipped. Claimed he didn't want no kids."

Kevin Jones split shortly before I was born. He only showed up to sign my birth certificate because my uncle Mike threatened him to do so. There was no love loss between my sperm donor and me. I didn't really care that he wasn't there for me, because I had my O.G. looking out for me and my mama. Now, finding out I have a brother I never got a chance to know growing up, filled me with rage toward Kevin. I felt like murking him.

"Fuck that nigga. It is what it is. We blood." I took what he told me at face value. My dawg, Yuriah, didn't surround himself with snakes. So anybody in his inner circle was rock solid. Then, the few times I had been around Kamal, his personality and swag told me he was trustworthy.

"What do we do now?" he asked me. I knew he was feeling just as vulnerable as I was feeling. It wasn't everyday a person was told they had a brother they knew nothing about. His value and beliefs in family ran just as deep as mine, so I knew he was in his mental too.

I stared at him so he could see the intensity in my eyes and my resolve. "Now we move forward. I am my brother's keeper." I held out my fist. My brother had a right to everything that I had. I knew he had his own, but he was my blood and I looked out for my own. He had a niece and nephew he didn't know and vice versa for me.

His fist bumped mine. "I am my brother's keeper."

Chapter 10

Loyalty and friendship, which is to me the same, created all the wealth that I've ever thought I'd have.

-Ernie Banks

Shaunie

Drinks flowed freely across the table. Me, Stacy and Nikki met at Landry's Seafood in the French Quarter. The hustle and bustle of the city could be seen and heard. Drivers honked their horns as they fought to get through the congested streets. Street cars ran in both directions. People walked up and down the streets. Some were tourists looking at the attractions and some were Orleanians getting off from or going to work at the surrounding businesses.

As the sun set, the nightlife of New Orleans was unrivaled. Our city's entertainment ranged from clubs and sailboat rides to tours of the infamous cemeteries. Several blocks from the restaurant, the noise from Bourbon Street would be heard as soon as we stepped out the door.

Nothing compared to my city and the people. Our culture was rich, filled with major historical elements. The cuisine was known worldwide. Many cities tried to mimic New Orleans flavors or New Orleans originality, but never replicated it the way we do.

"Thank y'all so much for taking on the task of keeping the daycare operational. I couldn't imagine trying to work and take care of Keira, plus help Keyz. It's so much."

Nikki took over the role of director. She saw to the day to day operations. Stacy helped her at the center filling in the secretarial position. After the whole fiasco with Stacy sleeping with the doctor she worked with, she decided to quit working at the hospital. Killer still didn't know about her infidelity. She thought since she resigned and wouldn't be around the man she cheated with he didn't have to know. I didn't agree. What happens in the dark always comes to light. I didn't express my concerns after the initial time she told me. It was her life and she had to live with the decision. I had her back and would support whatever she decided.

"Girl, it's no problem. I actually enjoy working there. It's so different from working in the hospital. I love seeing all the little kids running around," Stacy said. Her eyes twinkled and a smile played on her face. I could see she still wanted a baby badly. Too bad Killer doesn't want kids. Stacy would make a great mother. She was so patient with them.

"Boo, you already know I got you. No thanks are needed. Anything for you," Nikki said.

A smile lit up my face. After all the years that had passed, we still said our motto. It was heartfelt. I would do any and everything for my best friend. We had been through some of our darkest and brightest times together. "And everything for you."

"So how is the physical therapy going for Keyz?" Stacy took a sip of her water, waiting for me to finish chewing before I answered. Me and Nikki were knocking back drinks, while she declined any alcoholic beverages. She was recovering from a stomach bug that she caught at the daycare. Not taking a chance that the drinks wouldn't sit well in her stomach, she drank water. Being around a bunch of kids all day everyday would make even a person with a strong stomach sick. Many of the kids had runny noses that they would use their hands to wipe. Then they would touch another person. They were germ magnets.

Keyz had made some major progress, but we were keeping mum about it. We weren't really sure what to expect and how far his progress would be. Until we had a definite answer, we were just playing it by ear and taking it day by day.

"He is doing real good. Ramon keeps him busy working his upper body strength and slowly taking small steps with the bars. I'm proud of the way he's endured. It took him a minute to get in a better place, but he's there and moving forward. A lot of people would have just given up and willed themselves to die. He tried that shit, but I wasn't having it." We have too much to live for for him to give up.

"Living paralyzed is life changing. I have seen so many people go through it while working at the hospital."

"It is life changing, but you are still living. Nothing changes in your life. What changes is the way you live your life. Some people aren't that fortunate. He is still surrounded by people who love and care for him. I'm just glad he moved forward with his life and decided to make the best of it."

"I know that's right. When life throws you lemons you gotta make lemonade with them bitches and add some vodka. Keeping it moving," Nikki said. Her ass was drunk. We couldn't help but to burst out laughing at her.

We ate our salad as we waited on our entrees. The talk about what was happening in our lives resumed. We had to play catch up.

I asked Nikki about Thugga and that soured her mood. She signaled the waitress to bring her another drink. "I don't know and I don't care. Thugga can kiss my ass and go on about his business. We don't have shit to talk about. Anything about Lil' Thugga can go through his mama. I am fucking done with him. There is no Nikki and Thugga. He didn't want me when he had me and I damn sure don't want him now. I still love him, but I love me more. Fuck him."

Her rant ended any and all talk about Thugga. She was adamant about not messing with him anymore. The vehemence in her voice was evident. I guess it really was the end of them, at least on her part. I was so sure that she would have given in by now. However, I respected the hell out of her for moving on and focusing on herself. The break-up wasn't easy, but she didn't let it break her.

"Enough about me." Nikki turned to Stacy with a smirk on her face. "How is operation baby coming with Killer?"

The happy expression on her face transformed to a crestfallen look. I felt her sadness from across the table. "It's not going to happen. That nigga even started using condoms and watching me take my birth control pills in the morning. He acts like I'm going to trap him or some shit."

Reaching over the table, I grabbed her hand and gave it a squeeze. "I'm sorry, honey."

"I can't take it anymore. I just want a baby with the man I love and who claims to love me. What's wrong with that? I want to be a mother some day and I don't think it's ever going to happen with Killer. But enough of the sad, sappy stuff. We are out enjoying ourselves. Let's hit Bourbon Street before we go home."

We talked about Keira's upcoming birthday. My baby was turning three. I hadn't planned on giving her a party because we had so much going on. My girls convinced me that a party was just what we needed. I couldn't disagree after I thought about the many changes we went through.

My name being called from across the dining room of the restaurant interrupted us. I looked in the direction of the voice and saw Jamal strutting over to our table. He was dressed in stone washed ripped skinny jeans and a babydoll white shirt. Cute strappy scandals were on his feet. His black hair was cut in a Mohawk with layers falling to the side. His make-up was beat. Jamal might have been born a man, but he sure knew how to style like a woman. He dressed better than some chicks I ran across.

"Hey Jamal," I said when he approached the table.

He bent over and gave me a quick hug. "Hey boo. Look at you looking all cute with your beautiful self." His hand waved over me to emphasis his point. "Hey ladies. How y'all doing?" he addressed Stacy and Nikki. They waved at him and said hey.

"I see you on fleek. You looking good, honey," I told him.

"Aren't I tho'?" He spun in a circle so I could see what he looked like from all angles. My eyes rolled upwards before I could stop them. Dramatics followed him everywhere. "Anyway, I saw you sitting here and I just wanted to say I'm so sorry to hear that Keyz was injured. I'm praying for his recovery and your family."

"Aaaawwww. Thank you, Jamal. I appreciate that."

"Honey, it's no problem at all. I'm here for you. Let me know if you need help giving Keyz a sponge bath. I'm more than willing to help." He looked so sincere, but his battling eyelashes told me he was trying to get a laugh from me and he succeeded. He could never pass up the chance to say something about Keyz.

We burst out laughing at his comment. I didn't take offense because that was just Jamal's way of joking around. He had been around Keyz a time or two in the club and he never said a thing out of line. "I'll make sure I keep that offer in mind."

"Alright boo. Let me get on up out of here. See you next week." As Jamal walked off, the waitress finally came with our entrees. She placed our food on the table, asked if we needed anything then walked away.

We dug in our food while keeping the conversation going. After several bites of my food, I felt my stomach bubbling. I had a few drinks without eating. I took a sip of water to try and calm it.

A wave of nausea came over me. The water I just drunk was churning in my stomach. Bile rose up. I jumped up from my seat and made a mad dash to the restroom. Flying in the stall, I retched. The liquid and food I ate rolled up my throat and came out in one long purge, followed by another ten seconds later. When I was done, I sat on the floor of the restroom to get my bearings. As I sat there thinking, I realized I hadn't had a period in a few months. The stress of dealing with Keyz and the kids made me lose track of it. A nagging suspicion settled in the back of my mind. First thing in the morning I was going to see my doctor. But in my heart, I knew and I didn't really need a doctor to confirm what my heart already knew.

Nikki Tee

Chapter 11

The whole point of loyalty was not to change: stick with those who stuck with you.

-Larry McMurtry

Keyz

The room was filled to capacity with just about every worker on my roster. Some of the higher ranking workers sat and others stood. The men standing formed a line along the walls. I looked down the length of the table that sat twenty. The different faces stared at me, expectantly. For weeks rumors buzzed around the city about my disability. Though unspoken, I knew many wondered about my ability to handle my empire while being paralyzed.

I sat at one end of the table facing the door. Briefly acknowledging several members at the table, I called order in the room by tapping my fingers on the table to gain everyone's undivided attention. Having leaned back in my chair, I got down to business.

"As you all know, the threat to the team has been eliminated. The threat was posed by King and Qwan."

Someone, I knew not who, murmured "fuck nigga" under his breath. Many of the niggas on my team felt some kind of way about Qwan being a traitor. It was hard to believe that a nigga who went hard for the team was involved in the betrayal. That nigga's acting skills were worthy of an Oscar.

"Y'all held it down when I was out. I appreciate all the hard work and dedication to the team." My crew nodded their heads. They didn't speak out, but waited for me to continue. "It's back to business and it's time to expand." I saw the surprise on their faces. They didn't expect me to be making boss moves and changing much since they thought I was paralyzed. Only my closest crew knew about the progress I was making.

"What type of expansion are we looking at, boss?" Hassan asked from his spot at the table.

I got in touch with Alejandro yesterday and he put me on game. The dude that used to cop from him from Baton Rouge was looking at life in prison because he was a three time felon. The law was going to put that nigga under the jail. He wasn't going to see the light of day no time soon. That info provided me the opportunity to get more territory. I told Alejandro my thoughts and he gave me some useful advice. We cut a deal for more product. Since I was going to be copping more coke, he cut the price per key.

"The city of New Orleans is already mine. We need more territory for our operation. Slidell and Baton Rouge are going through a drought since the raids last year. The Feds rounded up the cities' dealers, but there is money to be made there."

After I spoke with my connect, I called an emergency meeting with Rayne, Thugga, and Killer. I put them on game and we unanimously agreed to make moves in BR and Slidell. I didn't need their agreement because I was the boss and it was my empire, but I had mad respect for my niggas and wanted to hear their thoughts.

"Some of you will be temporarily relocated to get the new areas up and running. Your job will be to keep watch for any new potential recruits, but to also keep the money rolling in from the new traps."

At the mention of relocation several workers shifted in their chairs and scuffled their feet. Nobody wanted to leave the city for a back water city.

I decided to offer an incentive to entice them. "Any and all who relocate have the opportunity to run your own trap, in my stead, of course." Ears perked at that opportunity. I noted several younger soldiers, who didn't run traps, stood a little taller.

"What about backlash?" One of the younger soldiers, who I didn't instantly recognize, asked. He stepped forward so that I could see him and answer his question.

"Any and all threats must and will be eliminated."

"That could start a turf war," someone else said.

I put both of my hands on the table and pushed myself up into a standing position. My upper body held me up with support from the table. Slowly, but surely, I was gaining my mobility back. Finally on my feet, I stood before my crew. Surprise showed on their faces as they paused and looked at me. Last they heard, I was paralyzed from the waist down and wouldn't walk again. "Then we will be waiting."

My legs trembled from standing so long, but I refused to show weakness in front of them. After several more minutes of standing and looking each nigga in the eye, I lowered myself back to my seat. The relief was instant, but my facial expression didn't alter.

Several of my members had questions about how we were going to proceed. I gave them some info, but didn't outline all the info or details. We went over monthly reports and made adjustments where needed. Then I called the meeting adjourned.

"Hassan, I need to holla at you, dawg," I told him when he stood to leave. My inner crew remained in the seats to the left and right of me. He gave me a questioning look before he sat back down and waited for the room to clear out.

A few months back I took notice of how ambitious Hassan was. I had been peeping game for a minute. For the last two years the lil' young'un climbed the ladder. I respected his hustle.

"What's up, boss?"

"I want you to handle the startup of the B.R. op." My inner crew was vital to my main operation here in the N.O., so they were staying put. Plus, I didn't trust no other muthafuckas to surround me. There was no shade from them about not heading one of the new cities, because they were cool where they were. There was no need for greed, because we were all eating.

His mouth dropped open. Recovering quickly, he said, "Man, I don't know what to say. I'm down with it. Thanks, boss man."

"No need to thank me. You proved yourself capable. But don't fuck up. You will get no second chance. You will be held accountable for every soldier's action. You up to that?"

"Yeah, boss. I'm up to it."

"Cool. Now, Rayne will be making weekly runs to B.R. to collect profits. Killer gon' locate trap houses and Thugga is going to be the go to person. Same as here. Nothing changes, but the location."

After hitting it up and answering his questions, he left. Rayne and Killer followed shortly behind, leaving me and Thugga alone.

He was my ride to the meeting spot. I could stand on my legs for a few minutes unassisted and could even take a few steps, but I was nowhere near being ready to drive on my own.

Thugga had been my friend the longest. I trusted Killer and Rayne with my life in a shoot-out, but Thugga was the only one I trusted to see me at my weakest in public. I needed to walk with a walker to move around without my wheelchair. My pride wouldn't allow me to let my crew see me that way. I wasn't complaining though, because that was better than being laid up in the bed.

He walked over to the closet door and took out the walker. When he reached me, he unfolded it and placed it next to my chair. "Thanks, man."

"Cut that thanks shit out, my nigga." I pushed myself forward in the chair, took hold of the handles, and stood up carefully. When I felt comfortable, I began walking toward the door. My dawg followed closely behind, in case I needed help.

He walked ahead to open the door for me. I maneuvered myself into the car unassisted. Thugga popped the trunk and put the contraption in then got in the driver's seat.

We listened to the radio as we drove around the city a bit. I wanted people to see my face while I was out and about.

"How you feeling, man?" Thugga asked me.

"It feels good to be back in action. That staying in the house shit is for the birds. I ain't used to staying put. My therapy is getting me back on track."

"Dawg, I gotta say, I'm glad you made it out the shooting alive. I couldn't lose my homie."

"Shid. I wasn't ready to be gone," I chuckled and he joined me.

I wasn't ready to die. I had too much to live for. My empire was the way I made money to live, but I lived for my family. They were first and foremost. Family above everything.

Nikki Tee

Chapter 12

Through loyalty to the past, our mind refuses to realize that tomorrow's joy is possible only if today makes way for it, that each wave owes the beauty of its line only to the withdrawal of the preceding one.

-Andre Gide

Shaunie

"So, Ms. Williams, what brings you in today?" Dr. Bachaus asked when he walked into the room with my chart in his hand. He took at seat in his chair across from where I sat on the examining table.

I was naked from the waist down. Goosebumps covered my skin due to the climate of the clinic. "I've been feeling tired lately and nauseous. My period is a few months late. I can't remember the exact date of my last menstrual cycle.

He looked down at the chart. "Urine test results are positive, indicating you are pregnant. Congrats." He looked up at me. "Let's get you down to imagining for an ultrasound, so we can get measurements to get an accurate due date."

I nodded my head instead of verbally replying. With everything that was going on, I didn't know how to feel about expecting a baby. It's been three months since Keyz got shot and rendered paralyzed, so I had to be three months along. We hadn't been able to have sex with penetration, because even though he was able to walk around a little, he didn't get an erection.

Slipping off the examining table, I got dressed and went to get my ultrasound. I hated doing it alone, but I didn't want to tell Keyz until I was sure.

When I got to the imagining department, I had to wait ten minutes before I was called to the back. The whole time I waited I thought about my baby growing inside of me and how it would affect my growing family.

The tech instructed me to change into a robe and lay on the table. She squeezed cold gel on my abdomen. Then she rolled the probe around my belly, side to side. As she worked, she clicked on the computer, making note of my baby's measurement.

A strong rapid thumping sound filled the room when the tech picked up on my baby's heartbeat.

"What a strong heartbeat," the ultrasound tech said, not looking away from the screen. Tears filled my eyes listening to the life growing inside of me. *I wish Keyz was here to share this moment with me.* Blinking away the tears of happiness, I stared at the screen in amazement. I couldn't tell what was what, but I clearly saw a little baby developing.

Pulling me from my daze of happiness, the tech removed the instrument and the room seemed quiet without the rhythm that just had me captivated. "All done, Ms. Williams. I will send these results upstairs in a minute. You can go back to Dr. Bachaus' office now to review them with him. Congrats," she said. She handed me a towel and exited the room to give me privacy to change back into my clothes. The tech left pictures of the sonogram on the table for me.

I used the towel to wipe myself off before I got dressed. Picking up the pictures, I held them in my hand and just stared in wonder. Bending down, I kissed the image then put them in my purse.

The nurse directed me to the room I had previously occupied. Dr. Bachaus came in immediately.

"Based on the measurements, you are approximately sixteen weeks pregnant. Here is a prescription of some prenatal vitamins. It's very important that you take them every day. I'll see you back in a month." He give me the prescription and walked out the door.

I sat in shock. When the doctor said I was four months, I backtracked and did the math. Four months ago, Keyz and I got back together. But before we got back together, I was sleeping with Dam, on a regular.

Bile rose in my throat as a flashback flowed to my mind. Around the date of conception, I had sex with Keyz and Dam only hours apart. It wasn't planned, it just happened that way. A wave of dizziness threatened to overwhelm me with the implication. The episodes of Maury that I used to watch played in my mind, except I was on the show with both possible fathers. *You are not the father echoed rung in my ear, over and over again.*

Just when everything was going great for me and my man, more bad news developed. My hands were clammy and my heart rate accelerated. *"How am I going to tell Keyz?"* was my last thought before I fainted.

***

A cloud of anguish followed me everywhere the past few days after I got the news of my pregnancy. What should have been a happy time in my life was ruined with doubt. I went from only being with one man to having a baby and not knowing who was the father of my unborn child. Jumping from dick to dick, I felt like I was playing thot scotch. It's funny how I used to be so judgmental and talk about other women who faced the dilemma I was now in. I never thought I would be that woman. The saying "never say never" had never seemed so profound until now. I completely understood, because I was now like the women I used to look down on and judge.

Physical and mental exhaustion made me lean back in the seat and close my eyes. My appointment was ten minutes ago, but I couldn't force myself to get out the car. It was hard hiding my morning sickness from Keyz. I got up several hours before he did so he wouldn't notice. Keeping up with pretenses were hard. I didn't tell him about the baby because I knew I had to get rid of it. The thought of killing another baby was so hard, but I just couldn't go through life not knowing. Many women would have just passed the baby off as their man's kid. Keyz would never doubt it, but I couldn't do him like that.

I sat in the car for what seemed like hours, contemplating what I needed to do. "God, please guide me," I said to no one. The gray building loomed in front of me. I stared at it with dread before I turned my head away. The tinted glass windows and beautiful modern design of the building belied the horrors of what went on inside. Developing babies were ripped away from the protective wombs of the women who were supposed to cherish them. The air suddenly seemed heavy and I couldn't get enough oxygen into my lungs.

Seeing this building made me confront a memory that I had buried. It had haunted me for months until I was able to suppress it in order to survive and live with the decision I had made. My abortion was traumatic. The pain was excruciating. It felt like someone was ripping apart my insides. But then again, that's exactly what happened. A part of me was ripped away. It was an experience that I never wanted to live through again, but here I was.

A tear fell, but I quickly wiped it away. There was no way I could have this baby, no matter how much I wanted to. I just had to learn to live with the decision. Getting myself together, I regulated my heartbeat and breathing by taking calming breaths. Making up my mind, I put my RayBans on to hide that I had been crying. I grabbed my purse from the passenger seat and pushed opened the door.

Finally, I got out of my car and approached the building. The sun was dimmed by clouds that covered it. The clouds were dark and looked full to bursting, releasing giant tears. I couldn't help but compare them to my emotions. I reached for the door. My heart raced and nausea built in the pit of my stomach. All I could think of was that I hoped I was making the right choice. There was no turning back.

Chapter 13

We must not confuse dissent with disloyalty.

-*Edward R. Murrow*

Keyz

Rolling over in my sleep, I pulled Shaunie closer to me, her ass brushed my groin and a groan hissed passed my lips. Thinking I was dreaming, my hands slipped between our bodies and stroked. The feeling was so good and intense, if my eyes would have been opened they would have rolled to the back of my head. When I got close to busting, I jerked awake from my wet dream.

I opened my eyes and rolled away from my girl, laying on my back. Settling on the pillow, my eyes landed on the tent in my boxers. Surprise came over me at the sight of a full-blown erection. My morning wood throbbed. Springing it from the confines that contained it, I wrapped my hand around it and gave it a few strokes.

Seeing that my piece was working, I turned over and shook Shaunie. "Huh, what?" she asked sleepily. Her eyes didn't even open.

I shook her again. "Bae, wake up." Not knowing the next time my dick was going to get hard, I wanted to take advantage of the opportunity.

She swatted my hand away from her shoulder and fell back asleep. I fell back on the pillow. I started to just let her sleep. She had been so tired lately that I didn't want to bother her. My raging erection had other plans and I couldn't focus on returning to sleep with it.

Ignoring her pleas for rest, I pushed up her t-shirt, slipped my hand inside her panties and played with her clit. She moaned, but didn't fully wake up. Her pussy juiced up and at this point I went all in. My finger easily glided inside her. The wetness seeping out eased the way.

Turning to wake her up, I grinded my boner into her ass as my fingers worked. "Aaaahhhh," she moaned, pushing her ass back into me. "Keyz, wh…wh…what's going on?" she asked when she finally woke up.

"Sshhhh, it's okay," I whispered into her ear, trying to coax her to go with the flow. I lifted her leg up, but she turned away from me.

She sat up and looked at me with a wondering expression on her face. Throwing back the covers, she eyed my penis that was pointing straight at her, begging for some attention only she could give me. "Keyz, what if we hurt you if we do something? Should we wait until we talk to the doctor first?"

I looked down at my wood and back at her. My dick was saying "fuck the doctor" and I couldn't agree more. "Ain't nothing gon' happen. I have to feel that pussy now. I don't know when Imma get a hard-on again. Fuck that." At the indecision on her face, I pulled her down for a kiss. She opened her lips and I slipped my tongue inside. I kissed her until she started to moan. Breaking away from her mouth, I kissed her neck and ear. "Let me have some of that pussy," I whispered in her ear before I stuck my tongue in her ear. With little pants, she nodded. "Turn on your side."

She turned over to her side without hesitation, wanting completion just as much as I did. I ran my hand up and down her bare legs before I lifted it up. When she opened her thighs wider I slipped right in.

"Yes!" she exclaimed when I penetrated her to the hilt. "Aaaahhh, Aaaahhh."

My left hand tangled in her hair. I tilted her head backwards. My right hand squeezed her firm tits as my hips pistoned into her warm, wet opening. Her juices flowed from her body, forming a puddle in the bed. "Aaaaw fuck, bae. This pussy so good." I increased my pace. I felt my nut building. "Damn, bae, I miss this good shit right here."

Our passion created a sheen of sweat on our bodies. My chest and torso rubbed against her back as I fucked her like there was no tomorrow. "Keyz, don't stop. Fuck meeeeee."

My hand tightened in her hair and my other hand squeezed her breast real hard. So caught up in the moment, I didn't realize how rough I was being. She didn't say anything, so I guess she was enjoying it too.

"I'm about to cum." My pace double timed and I was hitting her in spots I hadn't felt before. It felt like I was hitting her uterus.

"I'm cuuuumiiin," she screamed a long moan. Her muscles tightened on me and sent me over the edge. My release shot through my shaft, filling her up. My dick throbbed for long seconds until my nuts was emptied.

We both exhaled loudly when I was done. She turned over to face me and smiled a radiant smile. "You were a beast. I don't remember us ever fucking like that."

I tried to catch my breath from the exertion. "I ain't never gone three months without your pussy. That's why I had to beat it up. Your shit is good, bae. I missed that pussy wrapping around me like a glove. Come here."

I pulled her to me and pushed her head to my chest. She yawned and twisted a little to settle.

"Ouch." She placed her hand to her stomach. I looked down to her face and saw a look of discomfort.

Concern quickly taking over I asked, "What's wrong, did I hurt you? Was I too rough?" I sat up.

She was quiet for a minute before she shook her head no. "I'm good. We just hadn't had sex in a long time and I guess it's a little tender. No worries." She kissed my chest then laid down.

I dropped the subject, wrapped my arm over her and closed my eyes. Sleep took me right after my head hit the pillow.

When I woke the next morning, Shaunie's side of the bed was still warm. She made it a habit of getting up before me every morning. I had hoped after the early morning when we made love that she would sleep in and we could have a repeat.

Having to attend to my hygiene, I slowly rolled out of bed. My dick was hard as bricks. Seeing it made me happy. My mobility was slowly returning and with it I hoped full control over my body. My steps were slow and measured as I made my way to the en suite. I pushed opened the bathroom door with my dick in my hands, preparing to relieve myself.

I stopped before I walked all the way in. Shaunie was slumped over the toilet, retching. The smell of vomit made me gag. However, I moved forward to hold her hair away from her face. "You okay?" I was concerned for her health. She had been running herself into the ground trying to do everything for our family and me.

Not answering, she continued to vomit until she dry heaved. I rubbed her back, but she pushed me away. I backed away. She didn't want me to see her throwing up. I grabbed a washcloth from the cabinet and ran warm water on it. It was quiet in the bathroom once her dry heaving stopped.

Shaunie laid there on the floor for a couple of minutes, then dragged herself up and faced me. Her breathing was labored and tears fell from her eyes from the force of expelling the contents of her stomach.

"Feeling better?" I asked her as I held out the wet towel for her to wipe her face and mouth. My girl was so stressed and exhausted she was making herself sick.

She nodded her head, then cleaned herself. "Yes, I feel better now," she whispered. "God that was awful. Throwing up hurts." Moving around me, she went over to the sink to brush her teeth. Walking up behind her, I wrapped my arms around her waist and held her while she brushed and gargled.

The minute she was done she turned around and put her head on my chest. I placed a kiss to the top of her head. She stepped out of my hold and I released her. Grabbing my hand in hers, she pulled me from the bathroom and I followed her back into the bedroom.

We both sat on the bed. "I'm pregnant."

She spoke so softly I almost didn't catch what she said and still I had to be sure I heard correctly. "Come again?"

Turning to face me, "I'm pregnant, Keyz," she said more forcefully.

My mind raced from her revelation. I racked my mind trying to figure out when it could have happened. For the past three months my shit couldn't even get hard, less on get her pregnant. "Unless you the fucking Virgin Mary or some shit, your ass better fucking explain. We ain't been fucking, so what's up?" Shaunie's ass had been home everyday all day taking care of me and the kids, so I was confused and didn't understand. The only time she left the house was to run errands or to meet her friends and even still that was only for a few hours. No one really called her phone. Plus, the nigga she was chilling with was dead.

"I'm four months."

Instantly, my mind was at peace. My shoulders sagged in relief. A smile spread across my face. I cheesed up so hard my jaws hurt. "Bae, that good. I'm happy as fuck. Finally, some good news. We having a baby and I'm walking again." I pulled her in my arms. So lost in my happiness, I didn't notice her sad expression or tears that slowly tracked down her face.

She sobbed with her head in my neck. I pulled back with a frown thinking my comment had her upset. "I'm sorry, I was tripping. I didn't mean that shit like that. It was just out the blue and I wasn't thinking that you could be so far along." The crying continued and I sighed. "If you are worried about losing the baby, don't be. We know you are pregnant this time. I will get you the best of care. Don't worry, bae. I love you. It's going to be okay." The thought of another baby so soon after just losing one was a scary thought. She had to be worried about a miscarriage.

She looked up and her expression was devastated. "I don't know if you are the father."

Silence occurred after her statement. It left me speechless for all of two seconds before I exploded. "What the fuck you mean you don't know if I'm the father?" I jumped up off the bed. In my haste, my weakened legs buckled and almost gave out on me. I backed away from her and the bed. My anger was so great, I wanted to hit her.

Her hands clutched the comforter as if she was seeking support before she answered my question. If she didn't answer I was not going to be held accountable for my actions. I was liable to beat them from her. "When we broke up, I slept with Dam. And then you confronted me the next morning and we had sex too." She looked away. "I didn't use protection."

I paced the floor. Picking up the lamp, I threw it at the wall. She flinched and backed up to the headboard. "You fucked that nigga raw? You 'round here raw dogging with niggas?" In the distance I heard Keira crying. I ignored her cries. Answers are what I needed and I needed them now. Besides, I'm sure my mom heard the commotion. She'll get the baby and take care of her. "How could you be so fucking stupid and careless with your life? These niggas be having all kinds of STD's." Calling Shaunie stupid probably wasn't the best way to get answers, but I was on one.

Her tears stopped as her anger took over. If I wasn't mad I would have chuckled at the way she went from crying to mad instantly. Every time Shaunie gets pregnant, her emotions was all over the fucking place. They had a nigga walking on pins and needles because I never knew what to expect from her hormonal ass. "How the fuck are you going to stand there and call me stupid? How you mad? When we weren't together when I slept with someone else. Last I checked, you had a baby with a bitch while you were with me. Were you thinking of STD's?"

Just like a woman to try to prove a point by bringing up old shit she was supposed to have forgiven. "Don't try to bring this shit back at me. That hoe, Ashley, poked holes in the fucking condoms. I ain't never fuck a bitch without one. Fuck out of here with that bullshit. What you gon' do?"

The fight left her. I saw in her eyes how confused and scared she was, but my anger wouldn't let me feel sympathy for her. "I wanted to get an abortion."

My mind instantly repelled that idea. No seed of mine was getting killed again. Even if there was a slight chance the baby wasn't mine, I couldn't let that happened in case it was mine. "Fuck that. Your ass made your bed, now lay in that bitch." I had to get away from her before I put my hands on her. I walked over to the dresser and began throwing on some sweats.

Shaunie hopped out of the bed and came over to me. "Where are you going?" She grabbed my arm, but I jerked away from her touch.

I continued to dress then put on some shoes. "Move," I told her when she blocked my way.

"I asked you where you are going. Answer me, Keyz." I heard the plea in her voice, but ignored it. There wasn't anything I had to say to her. "Fuck you then. Leave."

Walking around her, I grabbed the door and walked out. Before I could fully get out the bedroom, she ran after me.

She pulled on my t-shirt. "Wait. Where are you going, Keyon?" she screamed and pulled my shirt harder, trying to keep me in the room with her. "Don't fucking walk away from me!"

I jerked away from her hold. She tumbled to the floor when I yanked from her grasp. I was going to continue to ignore her, but her cries stopped me. I looked back and saw her sprawled on the carpet, sobbing. "Get up." My voice came out more harshly than what I intended.

She cried harder. I felt bad that I treated my girl the way I was treating her, but I was pissed. People might say I was wrong and I was heartless, but until a nigga went through what I was going through, they couldn't judge me. I knew my ass was a hypocrite, because I had a baby on her. My pride was wounded and honestly my feelings was fucked up.

Backtracking into the room, I scooped her up in my arms and she quieted down. Placing her gently on the bed, I turned back around and walked out the door as fast as my weakened legs could carry me.

My mom was standing in the foyer holding Keira. When I reached them, I kissed my baby girl on the cheek. I saw disappointment in my mama's eyes. Grabbing my keys off the table, I left the house. My mama didn't try to stop me and Shaunie didn't come from the room.

It was too soon for me to be driving in my condition, but I didn't want to talk to, or be around, anyone. For hours I drove around the city, not stopping to holla at the many people who stared in the direction of my car when I passed by.

My subconscious must have been at work, because I found myself at the lakefront. Parking my car, I leaned back in the seat and put my head on the headrest. My chest was tight with emotions. Away from all eyes, I allowed the tears to fall. I was hurting so bad.

"Fuck! Fuck! Fuck!" I pounded the steering wheel with my hands until they hurt. Karma was a bitch. I was being served with what I dished out. Stepping out on Shaunie, I got another bitch pregnant. Now my girl was pregnant and I may not be the father. Only time will tell. Until then, I had to get my shit together and deal with it. The only reason why she had a chance to fuck someone else was because of my fuck ups. I prayed to God to let this baby be mine. My love for Shaunie was deep, but I didn't know if I could stand by and raise another nigga's baby. What nigga could?

Chapter 14

Don't let your loyalty become slavery. If they don't appreciate what you bring to the table, let them eat alone.

-Unknown

Shaunie

Keyz stayed gone the reminder of the day. Later that night when he did make it home, he came to the bedroom, saw me in bed, turned and walked back out the door. He didn't say where he was and I didn't ask. The next morning when I woke up, he was asleep on the sofa. I went back to the room, got dressed, grabbed my child, and left the house, heading over to my mom's house.

I wasn't going through no bullshit with Keyz again. I done put up with his infidelities, him putting his hands on me when I tried to break things off with him, got kidnapped and killed someone behind his ass. Now, here I am cooking, cleaning, taking care of his kids, and nursing him back to health and he tripping on me. If he didn't appreciate everything that I have been doing for him and our family these many months, then he never would. He could be by his damn self. I refused to stay in this relationship when we weren't equal partners.

Using my key, I let myself in my mom's house. It was early morning, so I knew she was in the living room watching the news while drinking her coffee. Keira was asleep in my arms with her head on my shoulder and my other hand was full, so I kicked the door to close it.

My mom met us in the foyer. "Hey, baby. What a pleasant surprise." She kissed my cheek then took her granddaughter from my arms. I followed her to the living room. She placed Keira on the sofa and covered her with a blanket.

"Hey mom," I said as I hugged and kissed her.

She sat across from me on the loveseat. "Y'all are up and about early." She lifted her eyebrow and stared at me. It was a question veiled as a statement.

Deciding not to prolong the reason for my visit, I told her what happened. "Keyz and I got into an argument. I needed to leave."

"Honey, leaving isn't going to solve anything. How many times have I told you that?" I heard how disappointed she was.

With a sigh of frustration, I lowered my head then looked back up at my mom. "We got into it because I'm pregnant and I don't know if my baby is by him or Dam. At this point, I don't care who the baby is by. It's my baby. Keyz is ungrateful. How is he going to be mad?"

The television played in the background. The sun peeked through the blinds. I played in my daughter's soft curls as I waited for her to say something.

She picked up the remote and turned off the television and silence descended over the room. Leaning over, she placed her mug on the coffee table before turning and giving me her undivided attention. "Now, I know you are not sitting there talking stupid."

"Mom, what do you mean talking stupid?"

Raising her hand palm out, she cut off whatever else I was going to say. "First off, congrats. I'm glad to be getting another grandchild. Children are a blessing that some people never get to know the joy of having. Second, you shouldn't be in the predicament of not knowing who the father of your baby is. You are old enough to take precautions and not get swept away with passion. Now, I know you are inexperienced and have only been with Keyz, but you need to remember these things. Everybody ain't clean. You lucky you got a baby and not an incurable disease."

I came to her for comfort and instead it seemed like my mom was attacking me and my character. "It wasn't like that..." I wanted to tell her that I didn't plan to sleep with both men. Keyz and I had broken up and I attempted to move on. He ambushed me outside and inside of my house. He pursued me sexually that morning. I was so caught up in my feelings of seeing and being with him again. In those moments I totally forgot about Dam and that we had sex the previous night.

"Uh uh, don't cut me off, girl. You came here for advice and comfort, but you are going to get this advice before the comfort." She gave me a stern look and I shut up. I wasn't going to disrespect my mother. "Don't beat yourself up over slipping and not using a condom. You aren't the first girl to forget and you will not be the last. Protect yourself. Lastly, Keyz is upset because he loves you and he is hurt that his woman is carrying a child that may not be his. The pride of men is as wide as the ocean and taller than a mountain. That anger is a cover-up for his pain. Give him time, he will come around."

She came over to me and wrapped me in her arms. Like a life-line, I held on to her. Comfort was all I needed. I was still shaken up that I almost went through an abortion to get rid of my pregnancy. As my mom held me, the confusion and fear slowly drained away and I felt my body truly relax for the first time since I got the news that I was pregnant.

No tears fell from my eyes. Me being all cried out was an understatement. Seemed like all I have done in the past six months is cry. My life used to be so full of happiness. Now, my life was always in shambles. In six months' time, I found out my boyfriend was a serial cheater, had a baby on me, broke up with him, lost a baby, accidentally overdosed, met someone else and slept with him, got back with my boyfriend, got kidnapped, watched my ex-lover get killed by his brother, watched my boyfriend get shot and be rendered paralyzed. I caught my first body when I killed Dam's brother. To top it all off, I'm pregnant and don't know who my child's father is. What a cluster fuck? I cried a lot, but what did I have to smile and laugh about? I wouldn't be in this situation if he wouldn't have been out fucking over me. The way I saw it, it was his fucking fault. I had nothing to be ashamed of. No commitment was broken when I slept with Dam. I was single. The only thing I was ashamed of was having unprotected sex. After I had a chance to think about, I was happy I was pregnant and didn't abort my baby. No matter who the father is, the baby is still my baby.

We broke apart and I gave her a small smile. "Thanks, mom. I needed that. You are absolutely correct too. I should have protected myself and not let my problems make me forget good sense, but what's done is done."

"And what about Keyz?"

"You made a valid point. I'm not agreeing that he has a right to be mad, I'm just saying that I can understand how he feels. We will get through it just like we get through everything else."

She nodded her head in understanding. "Y'all have been through so much in so short a time. Work it out if you can."

I grabbed my purse from off the side of the sofa and fished through the contents. "Do you want to see pictures of the baby?"

"Girl, you know I do. Let me see my baby." She yanked the sonogram pictures out my hand. I laughed at her eagerness to see.

My phone rang. I looked at the screen and saw that it was Keyz calling. Pushing the ignore button, I put my phone on the table. He ignored me last night, so I was going to ignore him now. I believe in equal opportunity. What's good for me, was good for him. Call me Petty Betty. Men showed their asses when a woman was always available, but got their minds right when you played their games.

We oooh'ed and aaahh'ed over the baby pictures. He called again, but I ignored it. My mom smirked, but didn't say anything. She knew it was Keyz calling from the ringtone.

Keira woke up and my mom took her into the kitchen to eat. I took the opportunity to call Keyz back. As if he read my mind, his ringtone starting playing right as I grabbed the phone.

"Hello?" I answered the phone with a snarky tone. Since having the talk with my mom, I was no longer mad at him, but he didn't need to know that. It never hurt to let a man grovel a bit. I would be lying if I said I didn't want him to chase me.

"Bae, I was mad okay. That shit was just a blow, ya feel me." I didn't reply. "Look, I need you to come ride with me to Ashley's house."

"Why?"

"Shaun just called and said she didn't come home and he is home by himself. I need you to come with me."

I rolled my eyes at him. He called because he needed me. "So, you wanna talk now because you need me for something."

I heard his sigh through the phone. "I was going to call you anyway. Damn right, I need you. You are my everything. I need and want you. But right now, I need to get to my son."

"Okay, I'm at my mom's house."

"I know. I'm sitting outside. Come on."

I hung up the phone and went to the kitchen. Keira was sitting at the table eating cereal. My mom was at the sink washing out her coffee cup. I walked over to my daughter and kissed her cheek. Then I grabbed her spoon and ate a mouthful of her cereal.

"Mommy, that's mine!" she exclaimed. I tickled her belly.

Turning to my mom I asked, "Can you watch her for a few? Keyz and I need to make a quick run."

She turned around, grabbed a dish towel, and dried her hands. "Girl, you don't even have to ask me to watch my baby. Go ahead. Take your time."

"Thanks. I will call you when I'm on my way to get her." I walked back into the living room, grabbed my purse, walked out the door, and climbed in Keyz' car. Without hesitation or reservations, I offered what support I could by being at his side.

We didn't say a word when I got in. He drove to go see about his son and I sat there as his support, like I have been doing since day one. I just wished I could get the same support from him when I needed it the most. A relationship should be about give and take.

From what I was finally seeing, we had no balance in ours. One person shouldn't do all the giving and one do the taking. We needed to have a talk soon, because I was ready to give him a wave and send him on his way if he didn't start getting his act together.

Chapter 15

So much of what is best in us is bound up in our love of family that it remains the measure of our stability because it measures our sense of loyalty. All other pacts of love or fear derive from it and are modeled upon it.

-*Harold Long*

Keyz

If it ain't one thing, it's another. I woke up and discovered that Shaunie was gone with Keira. Soon after that, Shaun called me saying he was home alone and was hungry. Knowing that Ashley left my son home by himself had me on ten. I was ready to beat her ass. Ever since Shaunie found out about Shaun, Ashley had been on some other shit. The crazy phone calls about being with her and trying to get me to fuck stopped after I beat her ass. We hadn't rocked like that since before she had my kid. Now, she was straight up reckless, talking shit and leaving my son home. The crazy shit was going to end today.

We pulled up to Ashley's house and hopped out the car. I walked to the door, with the assistance of my cane. With Shaunie at my side, I knocked on the door. No one answered. "Shaun, it's me. Open the door," I yelled as I knocked again.

"Bae, calm down. I know it's hard, but you don't want to scare him," Shaunie said as she rubbed my back.

The lock on the door turned. Shaun's little face peeked through the crack in the door. He looked scared, so I got down to his level. I visually looked him over for signs that he was hurt. "What's up, lil' man? Daddy's here to get you." He opened the door wider and threw himself in my arms. His body trembled.

"Daddy, I'm so hungry," he mumbled in my neck as I held him. My nose wrinkled in disgust when I smelled my son. He smelled like piss. That just fueled the fire of my rage at Ashley. With him in my arms, I stood up and it was a struggle with the extra weight due to my weak legs.

I pushed through the door and looked around the living room. The house was pretty clean. Shaunie followed along behind me. Her eyes took in every nook and cranny of the house.

I sat on the sofa with Shaun in my lap. "How long has your mom been gone for?" Ashley might be acting crazy with me, but I couldn't see her just leaving Shaun alone.

"I dunno know." He shrugged his shoulders. "I had to eat cereal the whole time, but I don't have no more milk and it got night time two times."

At the mention of two nights, Shaunie quickly looked up and gave me a look. I needed to stay calm to get some answers. That fucking bitch left my child for two nights.

"Who did she leave with?"

"Some lady. Daddy, can I come home with you and Shaunie and Keira? Mommy be mean to me and I don't like it."

I patted his head. "Yeah son." Deciding that I had enough, I said, "Go to your room and get whatever you want to take with you."

His bottom lip quivered and he looked sad. "You not gone leave me?"

Seeing him upset over the thought of me leaving hurt a nigga's heart. I ain't never seen my lil' man looking so lost. "I ain't gon' leave."

"Promise?"

"I promise."

He got off the sofa and ran to his room. I leaned back on the sofa, closed my eyes, and pinched the bridge of my nose. Ashley had to be found. I felt Shaunie moving closer to me, so I looked at her.

"Keyz, you do know you need to call the police, right? This incident needs to be documented."

"You know I ain't getting the police involved in my business."

106

"Listen, if you don't involve them it will be your word against Ashley's, if and when you decide to take Shaun. The courts are not going to take a child from his mother without proof of neglect. You have to do this to protect him. This may be the first time she pulled this, but it may not be the last. You can't strong arm in family court. Trust me." Her voice held no malicious intent. Some women would want their man to call the police to start up some shit with the baby mama, but her concern was genuine. She had a love for children, so I knew she only wanted what was best.

I contemplated what she said and I knew she was right. The courts did have a tendency to protect the mother's rights while saying fuck the father. It was all part of the plan to keep black men from being involved in their children's lives. The women used the family court like a shield while not realizing that they hurt their kids in the process.

Shaun came back into the room and we ceased discussing business in front of him. "I'm ready, daddy."

Shaunie looked at me and I nodded my head. She took her phone from her back pocket and left out the room to make a call to the police.

I played with Shaun on the sofa until she was done with the call. When she came back, we decided to wait in the car. I stood up from the sofa with a groan. Like a hawk she caught the sound.

"Come on, Shaun, let me hold you." She held her arms out and Shaun allowed her to pick him up.

We shut the door then waited in the car. I didn't know what Shaunie told the operator. Usually 504 take forever to respond to anything, but we only waited for thirty minutes. They pulled up and I got out the car. Shaunie stayed inside and waited, keeping Shaun entertained.

Two police officers exited the patrol car and walked over to me. I could tell the white officer was going to be a problem because his aura screamed cocky. He walked over to me, keeping his hand on his holstered gun. With all the unprovoked killings of black men like Samuel DuBose and Eric Garner by overzealous cops, I had to tread carefully. It was open season on black men. There was no hoe in my blood, but my woman and kid was ten feet away.

Sure enough before I can tell them what is going on I am asked for identification. I handed the white officer my ID and he went to the squad car, I presumed to check and see if a nigga had any warrants.

"So, what seems to be the problem?" the black officer, Officer Mercadel, asked me while his partner was in the car.

"My son called me and said his mama left him in the house by himself. I came to get him and he said he had been home alone for two days."

"Do you know where the mother may be?"

"No, I don't. I haven't talked to her in a few days."

The other officer joined us and gave me my license back. He hefted up his belt on his rounded stomach. His nameplate said Officer Boudreaux.

"Well, it looks like you are all clear with no warrants. Surprisingly, not even an arrest."

His partner turned and glared at him. What Officer Boudreaux said was entirely unprofessional and inappropriate. Some people couldn't hide how racist and prejudiced they were. Hell, he wasn't trying to hide it at all. I was beginning to think calling the cops was a mistake. This officer was trying to get a reaction from me.

Officer Mercadel continued to ask me questions about Ashley and Shaun. They grilled me for a few minutes then all of a sudden we heard tires squeal. I watched Ashley's car come down the street at a speed I was sure surpassed the limit. The car weaved side to side, movements erratic. Me and the cops jumped back in alarm when the car skidded to a stop at the curb where we were standing. Both officers drew their guns, keeping the muzzle toward the ground.

"Stupid bitch," I mumbled under my breath.

Ashley threw open the door and climbed out the car, with a bottle of liquor in her hand. She turned to walk, but stumbled. Clearly, she was intoxicated or high.

"Stop where you are," Officer Boudreaux directed her. She looked up and finally noticed we were standing there. Eyes bulging, she dropped the bottle and raised her hands in surrender.

He moved forward and slapped silver bracelets on her wrists. His partner used the radio attached to his shoulder to call the incident in. Ashley was placed in the back of the car. She started kicking and screaming, creating a scene. Getting caught red handed, she faced several charges.

Mercadel came back to me and asked if I had proof that I was the father. Ashley was not cooperating. I couldn't believe she would have rather Shaun get sent to DFS to a temporary home instead of with me. After I told him I didn't have any proof on me, but I was listed on his birth certificate, he told me social services had to be called to come out. He told me they had access to birth records and could verify that I was listed as the father.

The whole time Shaunie watched the scene through the window. Shaun had fallen asleep, which I was thankful for.

"He got that bitch at my fucking house. Fuck him and her. They can't have my child." Ashley's tirade was heard when the officer went back to the squad car.

Both officers stayed at the cruiser. I went back and waited in my car. Shaunie asked what was going on and I told her. She didn't ask anything else as we waited.

The DFS vehicle pulled up and an overworked looking woman got out. I got out and stood near my car. She spoke with the officers. Then she pulled out paperwork. The officers pointed to me and then she walked over.

She introduced herself before she asked to see my ID. Satisfied that I was who I claimed to be, she made me sign some forms. Then she said I was free to leave with my kid. I didn't even wait to see what happened with Ashley before I pulled off.

On the way home, I stopped at McDonald's and got Shaun something to eat until we got home to a better meal. He was so hungry he practically inhaled the food. Shaunie grabbed my hand and squeezed. I was visibly upset over Ashley's treatment of my son. First thing I was going to do when I got Shaun settled is call a lawyer.

We pulled in the driveway of my mama's house. I noticed her car was gone. It was a good thing she wasn't at the house when Shaun first arrived. She would have hit the ceiling.

"I'll go to the kitchen and fix something hot. You need to give him a bath," Shaunie told me.

"Come on, lil' man. Let's get you cleaned up and then Shaunie is going to have something good for you to eat."

He perked up at the mention of food. I gritted my teeth in anger. "Can I have some of those pancakes you make?" he asked Shaunie.

"Sure, baby. Anything you want. You can have whatever you like."

He ran to her and hugged her. She returned the hug before directing him to go get some clothes from his dresser in his bedroom. I went into the bathroom and ran some bath water for Shaun. He came in a minute later with his clothes. Placing them on the counter, he undressed. When he took off his clothes and revealed his body, my mouth dropped open in shock. He had mottled bruises on his legs and stomach.

The shock wore off and I lost it. "*Shaunie!*" I screamed. "*Shaunie!*" Shaun jumped when I raised my voice. He moved next to the cabinet and stared at me with wide eyes.

Footsteps echoed on the floors as she ran to the bathroom. She stopped in the doorway then placed her hand over her mouth as tears gathered in her eyes.

110

"Imma kill that fucking bitch." I wanted to cry like a bitch looking at my son. Failure rode my shoulders. I was supposed to protect him from everyone, but I let him down, allowing him to be abused.

I opened my arms for him to come to me. "Come here, son." My voice broke. He came to me and I held him. Shaunie dropped down to her knees and held him too. As we held him, I swore vengeance against Ashley for hurting my child. A child she was supposed to protect and cherish. I never believed she was the type of chick to hurt her child out of spite because of the father, but that was exactly what she did. All because I cut her off financially and only took care of my kid and paid the bills directly instead of lacing her account with money.

I stood up with my son still in my arms. Shaunie followed behind me as I walked to his room to get him dressed to take him to the hospital.

Ashley had better stay in jail or away from around here. If not, I was going to make her disappear. For good.

Chapter 16

Respect is earned. Honesty is appreciated. Love is granted and loyalty is returned.

-Unknown

Shaunie

Keyz pulled my hair roughly as he pumped into me with deep strokes. I was on my hands nd knees so that he could hit it from behind. My face was pressed into the pillow to muffle my moans.

He leaned over and covered my back with his strong chest. Whispering in my ear, "You got the best pussy, ma. It's so wet and tight. I can't get enough," all the while keeping up with his strokes.

I threw my ass back, signaling to him to pump harder and faster. Enough with the dirty talking, I needed sweaty, dirty actions. My hormones were all over the place and I needed his dick like I need air.

"Faster."

"You want it faster, huh? I got ya." Straightening back up on his knees, he held on to my hips and increased the speed of his thrust.

The faster friction built up my release. My inner muscles clenched on to his manhood. "Aaaahhhh, right there." My arms shook from holding myself up. When he hit my sweet spot, I came all over his dick. "Aaaaaaahhhhh." I released a loud moan that I was sure could be heard outside the bedroom. My stomach tightened like I was having a contraction. I forgot that having an orgasm during pregnancy the uterus contracts.

Keyz slapped a hand over my mouth to stifle the noises of our loving making and worked me over through my climax. When I was done, my body dropped. He was still hard inside me, but I had no energy left to keep upright.

"Man, what you doing? You fucking up a nigga's nut, bae."

I closed my eyes and yawned. "Shit, I'm tired." I tried to disengage him from my body, but he held on to my hips.

He grinded into me and it lit my desire anew. "I'm almost finished." Pushing my face down, lifting my ass up, he fucked me harder than before. I let the sensation wash over my body. Just when I was getting back into the groove, I felt Keyz stiffen behind me. His hot release splashed inside. Placing a kiss to the nape of my neck, he rolled over taking me with him.

I laid on my back next to him. My abdomen was tight, so I rubbed my rounded baby bump. I was almost five months pregnant. The kids were excited that I was having another baby. So was I. My mom was over the moon and Ms. Lynn was excited, too. Even though she knew it was a possibility that her son wasn't the father. All she had to say was, "You reap what you sow."

The only problem was, Keyz didn't mention anything about the baby. We tiptoed around the issue. He didn't offer any support and didn't ask about my health or any appointments. It hurt that he ignored the situation. I couldn't help but think he was going to leave me if the baby wasn't his. But I was cool with that if he did. After all the stuff we had been through together, one thing had become obvious to me in recent months: I was stronger than I knew. Gone were the days of my entire world falling apart because of the actions of one person. I love Keyz and wanted nothing more than to ride with him until forever, but if he chose to walk, I'd respect his decision and keep it moving.

A warm hand covered my hand on my belly, startling me. His big hand cupped my baby bump. In circular motions, he rubbed. My little baby fluttered inside me. I didn't think Keyz felt it, because he didn't respond.

He kissed my forehead. "Bae, I wanted to tell you thank you for having my back, like always. You stepped up to the plate to fill the role of mother to Shaun when you didn't have to. I appreciate it. I love you."

It's been close to a month since Shaun had been living with us. Keyz was granted full custody after an emergency hearing. Shaun's mother, Ashley, was declared unfit due to abuse and neglect. She called a few times when she was released from jail. Keyz told her not to come around and threatened her with bodily harm, the same she inflicted on Shaun.

"I love you too."

He huffed a sigh then leaned back on his pillow. "I know I have been an ass in the way I acted over the baby. I want you to know that I'm trying to get over it and be the man you need me to be. I promise Imma get better. Just give me some time."

I put my head on his chest. Being close to five months, we didn't have time to figure it out. Immediate decisions are what I needed. If he couldn't deal with the situation, arrangements needed to be made before the baby came. Instead of answering, I nodded my head. For now, I didn't want to disrupt the peace, so I left it at that.

***

After a few months of being away from work, I decided to drop by. Nikki and Stacy had been taking excellent care of my center. The profits where coming in and there was a major increase in enrollment. Kid's Kingdom was filled to capacity. Nikki had a natural talent. She stepped in and filled the role as director, effortlessly. By giving Nikki something other than Thugga to worry over, she blossomed into a very capable person who was able to step in and take charge. She was surprisingly business savvy. Being separated from Thugga afforded her the opportunity to see her self-worth besides that of wifey to a hustler. I had an idea to open another location and wanted her to run it.

When I walked in the building, she was on the phone. From what I could tell it was a parent. She ended the call and stood up to hug me. "You looking like you ready to come back to work, with your baby bump."

I sat in the chair. "I'm not in no rush. I know you got this." I missed being at work, but I had my hands full with Keira, Keyz, Shaun, and now the pregnancy.

"Why you didn't tell me you were coming? I would have ordered us some lunch. Stacy's break is in fifteen minutes."

"Last minute decision. I was out, so I just stopped by."

We discussed business and I told her of my idea to expand. She was on board with running one of the centers. I was ecstatic because I couldn't trust anyone more than her.

Stacy came to the office and hugged me. "You are glowing, honey." Going to the mini fridge, she got out a bottle of water. Nikki and I asked for a bottle. Even in the air conditioned building the July heat could be felt. There was nothing like a hot day in New Orleans. The humidity alone was enough to make a person have an asthma attack without ever being diagnosed with asthma.

Stacy sat down and downed half of her water. "Oh, before I forget, here." I grabbed a list from my purse and handed it to them. "It's the list for what you are responsible to arrange for Keira's birthday party." Every year, we delegated things to do for the kid's parties so we didn't have to do everything on our own.

"Cool. I'm excited. My god-baby's party is going to be the bomb," Nikki said. She looked over her list then put it in the drawer. "I'm going to start tomorrow."

Stacy used a pen to mark on her paper. "This should be easy enough. I know one vendor who can provide most of the equipment." She rubbed her belly and sighed.

"Don't tell me you are getting sick again? The kids wearing you down? That two-year-old class is a handful." I noticed the bags under her eyes and she appeared tired.

"It's not the kids. I'm pregnant." She smiled. It was the brightest smile I had seen from her in a long time. I was happy for her. She had wanted a baby for the longest.

Water spewed out of Nikki's mouth. She got up and threw the water away. Puzzled at her behavior, we looked at her funny.

"What's wrong with your crazy ass?" Stacy asked her.

Nikki pointed her chin down and looked at us. "Both of y'all knocked up. That shit is in the water. I ain't trying for no baby." We laughed at her antics.

"I'm so excited for you. Our babies are going to be best friends just like us. I hope we both have boys." My baby was going to have a little cousin to grow up and play with.

"I just want a healthy baby. I'm eight weeks in so I'm still early."

"Well, congrats. I'll babysit my nephew anytime you want. I see you finally convinced that nigga to do right," Nikki said.

Stacy's face fell and I knew something was going on. "He doesn't know. The doctor said it probably happened when I was on antibodies when I was sick. The birth control pill failed. I took them religiously. Killa watched me take them every morning. I'm scared he is going to think I purposely trapped him."

I reached over and grabbed her hand. "I'm sure everything will be just fine. It's done now. He will love the baby just like he loves you."

"I hope you are right. He was pretty resolute about not having kids." She looked close to tears. I prayed she didn't cry. Two hormonal females together was a disaster. I cried and got mad all in ten seconds, without provocation.

"If he ain't alright with it Imma kick him right in his balls," Nikki said fiercely. We cracked up at her. Leave it to Nikki to make us laugh. That chick was certifiable. But I wouldn't trade her for the world.

117

Nikki Tee

118

Chapter 17

Loyalty...a will, a decision, a resolution of the soul.

-Pascal Mercier

Keyz

I walked through the alley to get to the backyard. Rocco came bounding toward the gate with a growl. When he saw me and got my scent he stopped in place to let me past. There was no tail wagging or looking for affection. He guarded the property and my uncle fiercely.

The alley opened into the back yard. My uncle sat in the lawn chair smoking kush.

"What up, neph?" He stood up and dapped me, pulling me in for a hug.

I returned the gesture. "Coolin,' unc. What's up with you?"

We sat in the lawn chairs. Rocca went over to his house and got inside, with his head out to see and hear anything.

"About to go over to Lorraine's once I smoke this." He hit the blunt and passed it to me, but I refused. Lorraine was a woman who my uncle saw off and on. Nothing serious. He couldn't commit. The one person he would commit to, his high school sweetheart, didn't want to have anything to do with him. "I see ya getting around better. Seeing you laid up fucked with me."

Stretching my legs, I leaned back and took the blunt. "Yeah man. That Rico Suave muthafucka is the real deal. That nigga had me back on my feet in months."

"That's what's up. Ya mama told me you and Shaunie got a lil' one on the way."

A white puff of smoke eased out my mouth and I groaned from the pleasure. "Yeah she pregnant. Almost five months along." I paused. I didn't want to tell anybody me and Shaunie's business.

She wouldn't appreciate me putting our situation on blast, but I needed some advice. Words to put my thoughts in perspective. Like the coke I pushed, raw and uncut was the way my uncle was going to give it to me. "The baby might not be mine tho.'"

"Fuck you mean, my nigga? That sounds out of character for Shaunie. I can't believe she would step out on you."

"Nah. It ain't like that. When she left me after finding out about Shaun, she started fucking around with this light-skinned nigga named Dam." I hit the blunt again then passed it back to him. "We fucked around too."

"Damn."

"For real. I don't know how to feel about that shit. I mean Imma take care of the baby seeing how the nigga dead and all. I ain't gone have her out here trying to take care of a baby by herself."

"You murked him?"

"After he felt my pussy, I wanted to. But check this shit out. That nigga was King's brother."

"Word?" I nodded my head. "Coincidence that they was fucking around or did he purposely check for her?"

Shaunie told me what went down in the room when she was kidnapped, so I knew it was just a coincidence and she wasn't targeted. "That nigga took a bullet for her. King shot at her and Dam jump in front of her. King basically confirmed that Dam knew nothing of it."

"What she got to say about the baby?"

"Nothing really. We don't really talk about the baby. Time will tell."

"Real talk tho,' she didn't have to tell you shit. She could have passed it as yours without worry. It ain't like you would have questioned her."

His words rung true. There was a lot of dudes raising kids they think are theirs, but aren't. "I know, but my head fucked up about it. I just don't know, man."

"What's there to know? She wasn't with you when she fucked ole dude and she around here playing mama to a kid you had on her. Ain't shit to know. Get your head out your ass. I know your pride wounded, but fuck pride. Pride will cost you everything, but leave you with nothing."

I thought about what he said. He was right. I couldn't alienate Shaunie or the baby. Taking care of the baby wasn't going to be good enough. I needed to put my all into it like I did Keira, with no doubts, even if there were.

"You right, unc, like always." I stood up. Rocco's head lifted at my sudden movement. When he saw I wasn't a threat, he settled back down. *Damn, I need to get my ass a dog. That muthafucka loyal as fuck.* "Let me get on out of here. I got business to take care of." I dapped him and hugged him. "Thanks for keeping it one hundred."

"Anytime, youngblood."

I left my uncle's crib with a new attitude.

***

Music pounded throughout the building. Half dressed women displaying their goods strutted around the Four Seasons, offering lap dances and other services. The coy aroma of perfume tantalized the patrons' noses, leaving a trail as they walked by. Their clothes left nothing to the imagination, but that was to be expected in a strip club. Several of the strippers eye fucked me, letting me know I could have them if I choose. Some even went so far as to approach me and told me outright. Skipping the bullshit, I wasn't with it tho.' This past year taught me too much to get distracted by pussy. Especially pussy that wasn't hitting on shit.

Me and my boys met at the club to chill and hang out. This was the first time I got out the house to relax since being shot. "Here's to making money and my nigga Keyz being A-1," Killer said.

With a clink of our Ciroc-filled glasses, we toasted before tossing back the alcohol. The strong liquor burned going down my throat, spreading through my body, warming my chest and loosening my limbs. It felt damn good to kick back and unwind after the constant drama that had hit me, Shaunie, and my crew from every side.

"The moolah is stacking nice as fuck. Taking over the other cities done put us on a whole new level. Soon, we are going to need more businesses to wash it. I think another strip club and a car dealership is the right way to go," Rayne said.

We took over Baton Rouge and Slidell after getting rid of King. No longer having a nemesis to worry about, I was able to focus more on my hustle. "That's what's up. Let's put this discussion on ice until Monday. I want to just chill." I needed a break from the constant discussions I had to have about my businesses. For the past month I played catch up with appearances on the streets and at my legit businesses. Work was the last thing I wanted to hear about."

"Niggas, relax. This nigga been fucking laid up and shit. Let's drink, smoke, and watch these hoes shake their asses and pop their pussies. Maybe get a lap dance or two," Thugga said.

I noticed he said watch the hoes, not fuck any hoes. That was a major step up from his normal behavior. He hadn't talked about any bitches since Nikki stopped fucking with him. To my knowledge, he hadn't been fucking with anybody.

We sat back, listened to the music, and chilled. Several women stopped at our table asking if we wanted lap dances, but we turned them down. I wasn't interested in no bitch grinding on me. Shaunie would hit the fucking ceiling if she got a whiff of another woman on me. I couldn't have my girl getting all hyped in her condition.

After several songs, a warm female hand rubbed my shoulder. I looked up and groaned when I stared in Sparkle's eyes. I hadn't seen her in a minute and seeing her now was too soon. She just didn't quit.

"Hey, Keyz. I'm glad to see you here."

I shrugged her hand off me. "What up?"

Her sidekick saddled up to Thugga and began giving him a lap dance. He looked bored, but didn't do anything to stop her.

Sparkle saw me looking at her friend giving my boy a dance and a smiled spread on her face. "You want a dance, Keyz?"

"Nah. I'm cool."

Ignoring me, she tried to move in between my legs and the table. I put my legs out to stop her from getting near me. Rayne and Killer chuckled. She stumbled, but caught herself on the table, righting herself.

I moved my legs so that they were hanging from under the table, preparing to get up.

She moved to the other side of me, opposite of the table, and whispered in my ear. "I can give you a private lap dance."

This hoe was like a dog with a bone. I was trying to control the impulse to tell her to fuck off, but she was taking me there. Opening my mouth, I was getting ready to lash out at her dumb ass when I saw sandals in my peripheral vision.

"Aaahheem." I didn't know who made the sound, but the clearing of a throat made me look up. When I did, my stomach knotted up. Shaunie and Nikki were standing right next to our table.

Thugga pushed the stripper off his lap. "Uh uh, nigga, carry on. We don't have shit to say to each other." He started to stand, but Nikki's words made him stop. Nikki was putting him through it.

The stripper stepped around him and walked off. Sparkle stood next to me.

Shaunie lifted her eyebrow at her, but still she didn't move. "You need to follow your sidekick and beat feet somewhere else," Shaunie told her.

"Keyz didn't tell me to go anywhere."

"I'm sure he did, since I saw him almost trip you. Besides, I'm telling you."

Sparkle looked down at Shaunie's obviously pregnant belly then at me like I was supposed to help her out. "You heard her. That's bae right there. Get lost." I wanted to push her away from me, but didn't want to put my hands on her.

Still she hesitated and opened her mouth like she wanted to say something. "Now, I know you heard my sister. Run along and take your business somewhere. She can't tag that ass because she is pregnant with Keyz' baby, but I can. Sluts get cut."

Nikki put her handbag on the table. Intervening before a fight started, Rayne stood up. "Sparkle, get your shit out the locker and leave. You were told several times to leave the customer's table. The customer is always right. You will not embarrass this establishment further with your desperation."

"You ain't my boss."

I didn't understand her persistence. I only let her suck me off and the bitch acted like she had a claim on me. My mind refused to even think about how the hoe would be acting if I would have gave her the dick. I dodged a bullet with this one. My whole night was turning sour and I was starting to regret even going out, especially coming to the Four Seasons. After all this time, I had expected Sparkle's freaky ass to go back to Chi-Town.

"You rather deal with Wynter? Because she is headed this way."

She looked over her shoulder and sure enough Wynter was walking our way. "Fuck y'all." She stormed away. Wynter looked at Rayne with a question. He gave her a nod toward the door, signaling for her to fire her and put her out the club.

The silence around the table was strained as we watched Wynter follow Sparkle to the back. No one said anything for a minute. I was waiting for Shaunie to pop off, but she didn't say anything. Thugga got up and went over to Nikki, but she grabbed her purse and moved away from the table and went to the bar.

The guys resumed drinking. I pulled Shaunie down on my lap. Burying my nose in her neck, I inhaled her sweet, clean scent. She leaned back and tilted her head to the side, giving me access to her neck. "What brings you here, bae?" I asked her. She had never showed up at the strip club.

"I came to check on you. This is your first time out chilling and I wanted to make sure the fellas are taking care of you."

I placed my hands on her belly and gave it a rub. "My niggas got me. I'm straight. Right fellas?"

"Shaunie, you know we got this nigga's back. I'm surprised Stacy ain't tag along with y'all." Killer smiled when he mentioned Stacy's name. He knew when one of us was around the other two weren't far behind.

"Stacy was already asleep when I called her. Otherwise she would be here."

"We got him. He is in good hands," Rayne said.

"I know. I just wanted to see by baby." She turned back to me. her lips were so close, I could stick my tongue down her throat. "I am about to go. I love you." She kissed my lips then stood. "Nikki drove and I know she ready to leave." She looked over at the bar where Nikki was ignoring whatever Thugga was telling her.

That quick kiss had me hard as bricks. I hung out for a minute with my niggas, but now that I saw my girl and knew she was missing me, I was ready to go home with her.

I stood up and grabbed her hand when she turned to leave. Turning to my niggas, I said, "Yo, Imma head out." Leaning over with my fist extended, I fist pounded them.

We walked over to Nikki to tell her Shaunie was leaving with me. She grabbed her bag and walked out the door, leaving Thugga at the bar. Poor bastard. I almost felt sorry for him, but then I thought of all the shit he did to her. I tried to warn him to get it together and not be so blatantly disrespectful. I guess the nigga didn't want to heed my advice since I had my own secrets.

Seeing the stuff Nikki and Thugga were going through made me realize how easily that could have been me. Sometimes I stop and think how lucky I am to have found Shaunie and for her to have stood by me through all the bullshit. I am one lucky man.

Not giving a fuck if they thought I was pussy whipped or not, I left with my girl.

Chapter 18

Unless you and your mate are united in purpose, dedication, and loyalty, you will not succeed to the extent you otherwise could.

-*Ezra Taft Benson*

Shaunie

My leg bounced up and down in excitement. A strong hand clamped on my knee, stopping the movement. I turned and looked at him. Keyz wore a smirk on his face.

"What?"

Putting his phone in his pocket, he said, "You over there shaking like you ain't never done this before."

We sat in the office of the clinic waiting to be called to the back for my sonogram. Today we were going to find out the sex of the baby. I couldn't contain myself. "I know. I'm just ready to find out so I can start buying things for the baby."

"When we are done here, let's stop at the mall and pick up a few things then I'll take you to lunch." He leaned over and pecked my lips.

I pulled back. "That sounds perfect."

We waited another ten minutes before I was called to the back. Keyz followed me into the small room to change my clothes. Reaching behind me, I tried to unhook my bra, but he beat me to the punch. I eased my bra down my arms. Keyz stood behind me and grabbed a handful of my tender mounds.

His grabbed a sensitive nipple and rubbed it between his thumb and forefinger, eliciting a loud moan from me.

"Aaahhh."

He turned me around to face him. His lips touched mine. I snaked my arms around his shoulders and tangled my hands in his dreads. Heat built as we kissed. Right when I was getting into it, he pulled back.

His mouth fastened over my nipple. I took in a quick, sharp breath. Pushing his head down to my breast, I fed it to him.

A noise outside the door made me freeze. My head snapped in the direction and I pushed his head away from me.

"What the hell? Why would you start with me?" I asked as I quickly took off the rest of my clothes and put the robe on. My hormones were on double time. I couldn't get enough dick. No matter that we had sex this morning.

He licked his lips and gave me a grin. My clit throbbed at the action. Keyz was definitely taking advantage of my pregnant sex drive. "I couldn't help myself. You were standing there looking all good, I had to taste you."

I shook my head at him. Securing my things in the locker, I closed it and turned to the door. We walked out the dressing room to the main sonogram room. The tech stood by the machine. She saw us and smiled. My face heated like flames. I couldn't tell if it was a knowing smile, because she knew what we were up to in the dressing room, or a welcoming smile.

She directed me to sit on the table and Keyz to sit in the chair next to me, facing the screen. For the next five minutes she clicked away on her machine. Keyz stared intently at the screen and asked the tech a question every time she clicked something new. The heartbeat filled the room. A smile lit up my face. Keyz turned to look at me and his face was a reflection of mine.

"Now, for the big gender reveal. Are y'all ready?" she asked.

I nodded my head, too excited for words.

"Bae, we about to find out what we having." Keyz grabbed my hand.

"Well, let's find out." The tech moved the probe several times before she stopped. There on the screen sticking out was a little wee wee. I was happy with either sex, but I always wanted a boy.

"Yeah man. Look at the piece pointing right at us. We got a lil' boy." He rubbed his hands, full of glee.

"Congrats on the baby boy, guys."

"Thank you," I told her as I sat up to go change back in my clothes.

Keyz got the copies of the photos while I went to the room to change back in my clothes. When I walked out, he was waiting at the door with the pictures in his hand.

He slung his arm over my shoulder, pulling me close to his side. "It's time to feed my boy."

Keyz and I did a quick lunch at the Cheesecake Bistro on Saint Charles Street before hitting the mall. Strolling through the mall, hand in hand, we hit all the children's stores. We picked up clothes for the baby and got the other kids a few things.

We passed by A Pea in the Pod maternity store and I wanted to pick up a few things for me. Keyz wanted to go back to a shoe store on the other side of the mall and my feet were beginning to hurt from all the walking, so we split up. I shopped in the maternity store for a few, leaving with some tops and dresses.

I walked to the food court to sit and wait for Keyz. Pulling out my phone, I sent a text to tell him where I was so he could meet me when he was done. Deciding to get a soda to drink while waiting, I went to the nearest counter and ordered a coke. Grabbing my drink, I turned to leave, but collided into someone as I walked away.

"Sorry." Looking up, my heart pounded in my chest. Dam's sister kneeled before me. She bent over to pick up the bags that must have fallen when we bumped into each other.

She straightened herself. "It's cool," she said before looking at me. Her eyes widened in recognition. "Hey, Shaunie."

"Hey, Damara. How are you?" I didn't want to stand there and small talk. So many emotions ran through me. From guilt because I knew the true story about her brothers' death to worry because I was very pregnant with a baby that may or may not be her brother's first and only child.

"I'm doing okay." She looked down at my belly. "Wow, I see you are pregnant. How far along are you?"

A lump logged in my throat. I cleared it before speaking. "I'm five months."

She did the math in her head. I saw the speculation in her eyes. "Is it my brother's baby?" She asked in a small voice filled with hope.

I didn't know what to tell her. False hope was not a good thing to cling to when trying to move on from something. There were doubts of the father, but I just couldn't force myself to tell her that. "No, honey. I'm sorry."

She looked away as tears filled her eyes. "You know Dam and my other brother died in a house fire. The fire department said faulty wiring. Apparently, it's been happening a lot after hurricane Katrina. It would have been nice to know we had something to look forward to to help with the grief. My parents are distraught."

"I heard about it on the news. I'm so sorry for your loss. Dam was an amazing guy. I cared very much for him," I said, meaning every word. He took a bullet that was meant for me. I would always love him for that alone. I pulled her in for a hug and she hugged me back for a second before pulling away.

Looking over Damara's shoulder, I saw Keyz enter the food court, so I wanted to wrap up the conversation. "Listen, hon, I have to go. Take care okay." I touched her arm.

"Thanks." She walked away and left the food court.

Trying to appear like nothing took place, I forced a smile. Keyz walked to me and I walked the rest of the way to meet him. He had several other bags in his hand. "Who was that?"

I wanted to tell him the truth, but I was afraid. We had been doing so well lately and I hated to bring up anything that would put a strain on us. He was excited about the baby and I didn't want to take that away at the mention of Dam. So I decided to lie. "That was a parent from the daycare asking me when I was coming back." The lie slipped so easily from my lips.

Guilt immediately replaced any other emotions I felt. We were starting new in our relationship with no secrets from each other. We had an open door policy to tell the truth no matter how painful it was. Yet, here I was breaking it.

"You can tell them you ain't going back for a while. At least until our baby is a year old."

We talked as we walked back to the table where I sat my bags. "Yeah, I hear ya, daddy." We discussed me returning to work after the baby. I pointed out that the baby could go to work with me. He wasn't trying to hear that.

I grabbed my bags and we headed to the car. While we walked, he struck up a conversation, but I only half listened. Keyz didn't seem to notice. I responded when warranted. I was too distracted from the thought of running into Dam's sister, Damara, and the high possibility that he could be my baby's father.

Nikki Tee

Chapter 19

If someone is loyal to you, they shouldn't be a thought, choice, or option. They should be a priority.

-Unknown

Keyz

The bed dipping several times in rapid succession made me open my eyes and pop up to a sitting position right before a little foot connected with my groin. In her My Little Pony pajamas, a giggling Keira bounced on the bed. She was dangerously close to bouncing where her mama laid, who by the way didn't wake at the commotion that was happening less than a foot from her.

Forgetting about the pain from getting hit in the nuts, I grabbed Keira and placed her on the floor next to the bed before she kicked her mama in the stomach. She squealed when I swung her to the side.

"Daddy, do it again!" she screamed in excitement.

I raised the covers over my waist to hide my boxers from her. "Keira, you can't jump on the bed anymore. You can hurt your mama's belly. "

"Because she got a big belly?" Her face scrunched up as she tried to understand. We told her many times about the baby, but she kept forgetting. Our family didn't have many babies or pregnant women, so it was taking longer for her to behave carefully around her mama.

"Yes, my princess. She has a big belly because she has a baby growing inside, remember?"

She climbed on the bed and sat on the side next to me. Grabbing my face in her hands, she asked, "How did the baby get in her tummy?" I heard a snort come from Shaunie, but I thought she was snoring. She slept like the dead when pregnant.

What the fuck? I thought. How was I supposed to answer that shit? I looked over at Shaunie to wake her up to get our daughter. She looked so peaceful sleeping, so I turned back to Keira who waited patiently for me to answer. I was in a state of panic over that question. Her question threw me for a loop.

Swallowing the lump in my throat, I racked my mind for what to say to her that was kid friendly. "Uummm, so you know how you and your mama like to put flower seeds in the garden and water it to grow?"

"Ummmphhh. We get lots of pretty flowers. I love the pink ones."

"Well, she swallowed a seed and now it's growing in her stomach." I leaned back with a smile on my face thinking I did damn good answering the question.

Confusion was written on her face. She tilted her head to the side and placed a hand on her belly. "But daddy, I swallowed a watermelon seed. I don't want a baby in my tummy." Tears filled her eyes and her lip trembled. "I gotta go to the doctor." She crawled over me to get to her mama.

Pinching the bridge of my nose, I sighed. My face was lined with frustration, not at Keira, but at my inability to answer the question. If Shaunie had to deal with these types of questions every day, it's no wonder why she is always tired and still didn't wake up with Keira patting her arm. I rubbed the back of my neck to relieve the tension that was building. "Keira, you don't have a baby in your stomach. Only grown-ups get babies when they eat a seed. Not you, baby girl. Little kids poop it out."

She paused mid pat to her mama's arm. "So my belly isn't gonna get big?"

"No, baby, it's not."

"Oh okay. But Uncle Mike has a baby, 'cause his stomach is getting big."

Not being able to help it any longer, I laughed. *Wait until I tell unc this.* This kid was too smart for her own good. She was so inquisitive and didn't stop until she understood. I have to remember to cancel animal planet. The last thing she needed to see was animals mating or giving birth. We would never be done with the limitless questions. Even though I was having a hard time answering her question to satisfy her, I was glad my baby girl asked questions. "Only grown-up girls can get baby bellies. Okay."

She crawled back to me and sat in my lap. "Okay, daddy. I'm hungry."

Glad for the change in topic, I kissed her head. "Go wake up your brother. Imma come and get y'all dressed. We gon' go eat some beignets."

"Yummy." She clapped her hands, climbed off the bed and ran out the room.

I got out of bed and headed to the bathroom. After releasing myself, I took care of my hygiene and went back in the room. Shaunie was awake. She sat up in bed. Her hair was all over. She ran a hand through her tousled hair. Her eyes were half-closed with sleep. She had never looked more beautiful to me.

Walking over to the bed, I leaned over and took her lips. I didn't care that she had morning breath. One taste was what I needed. "Good morning, beautiful."

She smiled radiantly at my compliment. Seeing the smile light up her face made me realized that I didn't compliment her much, tucking away a reminder to do so more often, I turned around to go in the closet to get dressed.

"I swallowed a seed, huh?" She said the last part with a raised brow.

"You wrong for that. How you lay there and let me fuck up that bad?" I asked while I threw on my clothes.

She laughed uncontrollably at the mention of how I answered Keira's questions.

I sat on the edge of the bed, next to her, to put my tennis shoes on. "Where does your daughter get them damn questions from anyway? Just last week she asked me why you scream for God at night."

"Oh, so now she's my daughter when the going gets tough." She climbed on my lap, straddling me. Her hands made their way to my head and her fingers stroked my dreads. The swell of the baby prevented us from being chest to chest. My dick sprung to attention at the warm contact of her core.

My large hands covered the cheeks of her ass and I caressed them, giving them a gentle squeeze. "Yeah, your daughter with her busy self. She stay into something and asking something."

"At least she has Shaun to keep her busy. Those two are conjoined at the hip. That boy is a mini version of you. Minus the attitude." A huge yawned escaped her. "I'm so tired. I could hardly force myself up."

I picked her up off my lap and sat her back down on the bed. "Get some rest. I got the kids." She slid back under the covers and put her head on the pillow. I leaned over and kissed her. Looking her in the eyes, I told her what was in my heart. "Bae, I love you. Don't ever doubt what you mean to me. You and the kids are my life."

"I love you too." She placed her hand on my cheek and held it there for a second. "You better go. I hear little feet coming this way."

Standing up, I walked to the door where the kids met me. I took them to their rooms and made sure they were decent. I put Keira's hair in a ponytail that looked like it was in danger of falling.

I loaded the kids up in the car and drove to downtown New Orleans. We walked a few blocks on Canal Street to get to Café Du Monde at the Riverwalk. Once inside, the kids pointed out the different shops and begged for everything they saw. We shopped at a few vendors and purchased knick knacks.

We walked the entire upper level then took the escalator down, straight to Café Du Monde. The kids ran to the counter, but I called them to a table. I sat the bags in the extra chair and waited as the server came to take our order. The kids played with a toy we picked up at one of the many stands.

About five minutes later, a waitress came over to take our order. She smiled at the kids before turning her attention to me. "Your kids are beautiful."

"Thank you." I ordered our beignets and drinks. While waiting for the beignets, the waitress brought over crayons and coloring sheets. I picked up a crayon and colored with the kids. Keira and I raced to see who would finish first. Shaun and I played tic tac toe. Competiveness was in my blood and it showed in my child. Of course I beat them both. Shaunie would let them win, but I didn't placate them that way. Fucked up as it was, it was a lesson to them to work harder to beat your contender.

The children didn't gripe about the fact I won and they loss. They were used to me winning most of the time. And I taught them how to not be a sore loser. Shaun and Keira decided to challenge each other. I took that moment to watch my kids interact with each other. Growing up with no siblings, I was often entertained by adults until I met Thugga and 'nem. Seeing Shaun and Keira talk made me think of Kamal, my brother I never knew I had. We missed out on having a relationship and building that closeness I saw in my kids. No time like the present, I was going to rectify that. We talked on the phone a few times, but that was no longer enough for me. I was going to hit him up later today and arrange something. Maybe a family day so the kids can meet their cousins.

The sound of the tray being placed on the table drew me from my musing. The waitress leaned over, too forward in my opinion. That much back wasn't needed to put the food on a table. She passed out the drinks and food. The kids dug in as soon as their plates were placed in front of them.

"Daddy, this is good," Shaun said.

Keira chimed in. "I know. It's yummy, daddy. Eat yours."

The server looked at the kids enjoying their food then looked at me. "Do you need anything else?" The question was simple, but her body language was throwing signals, which I ignored.

"Nah, we good."

"Okay. Let me know if you do." Her not so subtle tone implied she would be available for anything I needed.

Bitch, the only thing I need from you is my check, I thought. Here I am with my family and this broad acting desperate. It never ceased to amaze me how some women claimed that couldn't get a good man. Well, that's because a lot of them make themselves available to men who aren't available. I had to make sure I schooled my daughter on the game, so she wasn't walking around all desperate for male attention.

I ignored the waitress and began eating my food. Rolling my eyes when she finally walked away. The kids didn't talk while they chowed down on the famous cuisine. Keira and Shaun's faces were covered with the white sugary powder.

The waitress came back over with the to-go order I placed for my girl and my mama and the check. Once the kids were done, I cleaned them with napkins.

"Come on, Keke. Let's put the garbage in the trash can," said Shaun to his sister. He helped her from her seat.

She slid off the chair, but he caught her before she fell. "Okay. Sha Sha." His nickname she used to call him from a baby stuck. She could pronounce Shaun now, but still called him by the name she made up.

As they walked to the trash bin, I dug in my pocket and pulled out enough cash for the bill and tip I shouldn't leave that unprofessional hoe nothing, but I knew waitresses and waiters livelihood often depended on tips. Not knowing her situation, I left her twenty bucks.

The kids came back to our table. I grabbed the to-go bag and stood. "Let's bounce." They giggled at my verbiage. I grabbed

Keira's hand and she grabbed Shaun's. We both made sure our female was protected in the middle of us.

We walked out hand and hand. This was a moment to live for. It was worth everything a person goes through to have a single instance like this. A father spending time with his kids without the extra bullshit. My kids were happy and truly enjoyed each other's company and mine.

There was no drama. We didn't have to worry about being accepted, because we loved each other, flaws and all. All the bad things I went through the past few months was worth it. I would do it all again just for this moment in time. It was everything.

Nikki Tee

Chapter 20

Loyalty is the strongest glue which makes a relationship last for a lifetime.

-Unknown

Shaunie

"Put the cake on that table," I instructed Keyz, pointing to the table under the gazebo. I stood back with my hands on my hips. My back was killing me from standing and walking all morning.

Noticing my discomfort, Keyz stopped what he was doing. "You need to sit your ass down. Let the workers handle what we paid them to do."

I rolled my eyes at him. There was a major change in his attitude over the baby. He was accepting of the circumstances, which surprised me. Many men, especially ones with pride like Keyz, wouldn't deal with being with a woman who was pregnant and he possibly wasn't the father. He started coming to the doctor for my appointments and watched me to make sure I was eating healthy enough.

"Just move the cake," I snapped.

Keira's third birthday party was today and I wanted everything to be perfect for my little princess. It took me months to plan her party, with the help of Nikki and Stacy. Even with Nikki basically running the daycare, she still took out the time to help.

Her party was a carnival theme. I hired a clown to make balloon animals for the kids and constructed a big top for the kids to play in. There were popcorn, sno-ball, and cotton candy machines. Stacy arranged for the merry-go-round, the train and the space walk to be delivered early that morning. Workers had been setting up well into the noon time. Nikki made the party bags and party favors.

"Not on that side of the table. Put it in the center." The weather was perfect for a party. The sun was out, but it wasn't blazing. We set up tower fans in the tents to keep guests cool.

He picked up the cake and moved it to where I wanted it. "Bae, this is the third time you moved this big ass cake."

I special ordered a three tier cake topped with an elephant balancing on a ball. The cake served over a hundred people. I expected a good turnout between family and friends.

"This is the last time, I swear." My nerves were shot. I was nervous that something wouldn't go as planned. "Thanks, bae. I have to go and get the kids dressed. Make sure everything is in place one last time for me please." The party was scheduled to start in less than an hour.

Going inside the house, I stopped in the kitchen and checked the pans of food that were ordered before going in the living room where Ms. Lynn watched the kids to make sure they were out of the way as we prepared for the party.

"Come on y'all. Let's get y'all together." I told the kids who were engrossed with their iPads.

"I already bathed them. They just need to get ready. I'll get Shaun dressed and you get Keira ready. I ain't about to comb all that hair. She ain't gon' do nothing but cry with her tender-headed self and I ain't got time for that," Ms. Lynn said.

Keira covered her head with her hands. She stepped back and away from her grandma. "No, mommy. I don't want her to do my hair. I want you to do it." My baby looked close to tears. Before I could answer Keira, Shaun spoke up.

"Grandma, I'm old enough to dress myself. Y'all can go dress my sister." He puffed out his chest, standing straight and tall, trying to make himself appear bigger. A crisis or a disaster was always around the corner when dealing with these two kids.

I laughed at my lil' man and how cute he looked trying to look big and bad. He tried to emulate his father in his every action. Deciding to handle the simplest dilemma first, I spoke to Shaun. "I know you are a big boy, but I want to be sure you look perfect." His chest didn't deflate. He was dead set on dressing himself. "How about you dress yourself, but your grandma is going to just watch in case you need help," I said, trying a different tactic.

He looked thoughtful for a second before agreeing. "Okay. That's cool," he said, realizing that was the most I would give in. "But I'm brushing my own hair. Grandma's hand is too heavy and then if you move while she is brushing your hair she pops ya with the brush."

When he dropped the tidbit of info I looked at Ms. Lynn. She raised her hands in surrender when I arched my brow. I had no problem with her disciplining my daughter, but not for something she couldn't control. It was no wonder Keira cried when she mentioned combing her hair. My poor baby was only three and couldn't sit still the entire time it took to comb her hair.

"Boy, hush your mouth and let's go get dressed before the hormonal lady gets crazy." She took Shaun's hand and went into his room.

Turning, I went to Keira's room and she followed me inside. Her clothes were already laid out on the bed. She had pink tights with a colorful tutu. Her shirt had an appliqued number three. To complete the ensemble, she had hot pink Converse gymshoes and a matching bow.

I combed her hair then put her clothes on. Keira ran to the mirror to look at herself. "Mommy, I look like a pincess." She twirled and her tutu billowed outward.

"That's because you are a princess, my darling. Now, let's go to mommy's room so I can get ready. You can watch TV in my room."

"Okay, mommy, but don't take long. Daddy said I'm the guest of hon…" She cut off as she tried to remember the word.

"Guest of honor, sweetheart."

"Well, I can't be late."

We walked into my room. I turned on the TV for her, putting it on the Disney channel. When I got her settled, I took a quick shower and slipped on my maxi dress. Since the party was outside and I knew I was going to be hot and sweaty, I decided to forego complete coverage with makeup and opted for a light touch of gloss and filled in my eyebrows.

Stepping out of the bathroom, I noticed we only had five minutes until people were due to arrive. I sat on the edge of the bed to put my scandals on. "Come on. Let's go get your brother and grandma so we can wait outside for your friends to arrive," I told Keira, holding out my hand for her to take it.

Ms. Lynn was coming out of her room when we walked down the hall. "Look at my KeKe looking all pretty."

Keira blushed at the compliment and spun to show off her tutu.

"Where's Shaun?"

"Outside with Keyz."

I nodded my head and went outside. Keyz and Shaun were standing next to a table making a plate of food. I took a moment to admire the two men in my life. Shaun and Keyz were dressed alike with matching baby blue Polo shirts and Khaki shorts. Keyz had on Nikes and Shaun had on Sperrys.

Keyz saw us approach. He sat the plate down. "There's the birthday princess." He held out his arms for Keira. Just like a daddy's girl, she dropped my hand like it was hot and ran to him. He picked her up and kissed her all over the face.

Holding his daughter, he pulled me to him for a quick kiss. Shaun sat at the table ignoring us, eating his food.

The guests started arriving and the kids made themselves scarce when more children arrived. The party was in full swing. Keyz and his friends congregated on one side, talking and chilling, and me, Stacy and a few other ladies talked while the kids played and were entertained by the vendors we hired. The music was playing, but not at an obnoxious level that prevented us from talking and hearing each other.

My mom and Ms. Lynn acted like grandmas, as usual. Both of them walked around the yard talking to everybody then every few minutes going to check on the kids.

I excused myself from the group to check on the tables. Then I went to call Nikki to see what the hell was taking her so long to get to the party. Shaun kept asking for Lil' Corey. Just when I was headed inside to get my phone, I saw Nikki coming through the gate. Her arms were ladened with gift wrapped boxes. My godson trailed behind her.

She sat her gifts on the table that was set up just for that purpose. Lil' Corey ran to the jumping jack without stopping to say hi.

"That's my best friend. That's my best friend. She finna. She finna pop!" Nikki exclaimed when she got closed to me.

"Don't be talking about my big belly." I pushed her playfully before hugging her. Stacy joined the group.

Nikki hugged Stacy. "Look at both of my besties glowing. Pregnancy does the body good, huh?"

Stacy looked around nervously before turning her attention back to us. "I haven't told Killer yet, so watch your mouth," she told Nikki. I thought it was fucked up that she didn't tell his ass about the baby. But knowing how adamant he was about not having any kids, I wouldn't be shocked if he tried to force her to have an abortion.

I wanted to ask her more about it, but didn't want to talk about it here. It wasn't the time or the place. Nikki and I both nodded our heads to let her know we understood. We chatted for a minute then went to mingle with the other guests.

My baby ran to me every time somebody gave her money for a gift. She was excited about having it pinned on her shirt. Nikki and Stacy helped me with the games I planned for the kids. My mom and Ms. Lynn made plates for everybody who wanted to eat. Keyz stood and talked to his boys most of the time, except when Keira ran and pulled him away to show him something. He wasn't getting away from working, because he was in charge of clean up detail when the party was over.

Thugga kept looking at Nikki, but I noticed she stayed clear of him and didn't return any looks. I hoped them two didn't start no shit at my baby's party. My back was killing me from all the walking and standing, so I sat down under the tent to relax. I watched everybody interact and smiled. This was what life was all about. Being around family and friends, celebrating or just enjoying life. The only cloud in an otherwise perfect time was the absence of my dad. My dad would have been amazing with Keira. She will never know the moments of being with him.

Shaking away the morose thoughts, I stayed in the here and now. Keyz walked over to me. He sat in the chair before pulling my feet into his lap. He slid my sandals off and began rubbing my feet, not caring who was around and looking at him pamper me. No words were needed between us.

A moan of appreciation fell from my lips at the magic his large hands created. I leaned in the chair and closed my eyes. My whole body relaxed from that simple touch. "Thank you, bae," I said when he stopped.

He put my sandals back on and pulled me up from my chair by the hand. "Come on. Let's go sing happy birthday and open up these presents, so all these people can leave. Keira looks like she is getting tired."

I looked over at my baby who was sitting in her grandma's lap rubbing her eyes. The party had been going on for hours. With all the entertainment, time flew by. The party was a success and the kids played nonstop.

We sung happy birthday and opened the presents. Keira perked up really fast seeing her new toys and clothes that were gifts from her guests. I handed out the party favors to the parents and goody bags to the kids.

The guests trickled out the gate after saying goodbye once the party winded down. The company we rented the spacewalk and other equipment from came and broke down the things and left. My mom put the leftover food away. Ms. Lynn went in the house to bathe the kids and put them to bed. Keyz and his crew picked up the trash. Me and my girls took down the decorations.

Nikki took the décor and went to put it in the trash. Thugga followed her. I rolled my eyes because I knew their discussion wasn't going to go over well. I kept working and minded my business. I reached up to grab a streamer, but it was too high. Stretching on my tiptoes, I grabbed it. "Oooww." Bending over, I held my expanding stomach. I must have pulled something. A sharp pain shot through my stomach, but slowly went away.

Someone yanked the streamer from my hand. "Didn't I tell you not to do that? You are hardheaded young lady." My mom stood next to me with her hand on her hips. I rolled my eyes at her. She was a firm believer that pregnant women shouldn't do anything active. Often times, I argued that pregnant slaves still worked in the cotton field and they birthed healthy babies. But I didn't go into that with her again. The last time I mentioned slaves, one would have though I spoke blasphemy.

"I know, mom. I didn't think it was that high."

"Ms. Sharon, I done told your daughter to keep still, but she don't listen," Keyz said as he moved behind me, wrapping his arms over my neck.

"You need to make her go lay down, Keyon. She has been on her feet all day. That's not good."

I rolled my eyes at the both of them. They were discussing me like I wasn't standing there. "*She* is right here." I raised my hand up to get their attention. "So, y'all are going to gang up on me, huh? Well, you and your son-in-law can stand here and talk, but *She* is going to say bye to her friends." I left them standing there, shaking their heads at me and went over to Stacy, who was getting ready to leave with Killer.

"Thanks for coming, honey. I appreciate all the help." I hugged her. Killer left us alone to go holla at Keyz before he left.

"Girl, what? No thanks are needed. We are family."

"I know that's right. Anywho, we need to get together for lunch and to talk." I gave her a pointed look to let her know what I wanted to talk about.

She laughed nervously. "I know. I know. Let me go, girl. I'm beat." She walked over to Killer and tugged his arm.

For some reason I couldn't shake, I got a bad feeling about them two. Call me paranoid, but I felt it in my bones. I watched as Killer turned to her with a smile on his face. The love he had for her was undeniable. They left hand in hand. I pushed my feelings aside. *Maybe I'm tripping.*

I noticed Nikki and Thugga was taking long at the garbage, so I walked around to the side of the house where the trash cans were. My mouth dropped open at what I saw. Nikki and Thugga were making out. His tongue was down her throat like the cure for cancer was down there. She was pulling his dreads. I don't know if it was to pull him away from her or to pull him to her.

She opened her eyes and they widened when she saw me. I backed away, trying to not break up their moment. With a smile on my face, I walked back over to Keyz.

"What got you smiling?"

"Nikki and Thugga is making up."

Voices raised, the sound coming from where Nikki and Thugga were. Minutes later, Nikki came from around the side of the house, tucking in her shirt. She had a scowl on her face. I knew she was mad because she kept clenching and unclenching her fist. Thugga was right behind her. He seemed to be trying to stop her from walking away from him.

He tugged on her arm. She stopped and turned to him. They kept their voices down, but I caught a few words. Even though I knew Nikki was going to tell me everything that was said and happened, my nosey ass stood there, watching and listening. Keyz stood right next to me. Hell, everybody left stopped, listened, and watched. He must have said something to piss her off. She slapped the shit out of him. His head jerked to the side from the impact. He didn't respond in kind. The only thing he did was tighten his jaw and stood before her.

"I don't appreciate you accosting me like that. You can't fuck and suck your way through this. Not this time. Seducing me ain't gon' fix it, so stop trying to corner me." Nikki told Thugga.

"Don't act like you didn't just let me."

"Yeah, well. You caught me in a moment of weakness. Leave me alone."

He huffed out a breath and ran his fingers through his dreads. Looking away in deep contemplation, he looked back at her. "I'm not about to go through this anymore. I fucked up. Big time. I can't say I'm sorry enough for disrespecting you, repeatedly. There are no excuses, but give me another chance," he pleaded. A deaf person could hear the pleading in his voice.

Nikki stood erect, I saw the veil fall like armor, protecting her emotions. "I have heard that speech a thousand times from you. Nothing has changed. I'm not coming back."

"Look me in the eyes and tell me we are done for good. If you do, I promise I'll leave you alone."

My heart started beating faster as the soap opera played out before me. My emotions were all over the place. One part of me was glad that Nikki was putting herself first, but the other half saw the change in Thugga. Keyz told me he hadn't been with anyone else and that he was pining for Nikki. A person never misses a good thing until it's gone.

"I'm done, Corey. For good." Nikki looked him in the eye and told him she was finished for good.

Resignation was written on his face. He nodded, but he wasn't looking at her. He was looking in the distance. At the future he no longer had with her. He leaned over, kissed her cheek, and walked away. Leaving Nikki standing there. That was the end of Nikki and Thugga.

I walked over to my friend to comfort her, but surprisingly she didn't need any. At least not at the moment. We said our goodbyes and she went inside, got Lil' Corey and left.

Later that night Keyz and I lay in bed. The house was silent. Our TV filled the space with noise. My head was on his chest. His hands sifted through my hair. "The party was nice, bae." The deepness of his voice rumbled through his chest.

"Thanks, bae. It was nice. I'm glad everyone came. Keira had a blast."

"I'm glad, too." He settled down and drifted to sleep.

Not long after, I fell asleep too, thinking about all the memories we made today.

Chapter 21

We have to realize that there cannot be a relationship unless there is commitment, unless there is loyalty, unless there is love, patience, persistence.

-Cornel West

Keyz

"Don't let me fall. Keyz," Shaunie chuckled as I led her through the door of the suite. Her hands clutched my hands that covered her eyes. Her steps were slow and measured so as not to bump her stomach.

I walked behind her, keeping my hands over her eyes to shield her view. She was in for a surprised. I dipped my head so that my nose was in contact with her neck. I inhaled deeply, taking in her scent. "I got you, ma. I ain't gon' let you fall. You are carrying precious cargo." I placed a soft kiss to her skin.

We walked all the way into the suite before I dropped my hands. With the kids and the pregnancy, I planned a weekend getaway for us to relax. Our weekend consisted of being tourists in our own city. I surveyed the room at the same time she did. The room was the best a person could get at the Ritz Carlton on Canal. Candles were scattered all over the room. I ordered a fruit tray and finger foods for us in case we got hungry or if Shaunie wanted a snack.

Her gasp of surprise told me the room met her satisfaction. "It's so beautiful. Not that I don't appreciate it, but what's the occasion." Her hands rubbed her belly.

"I don't need an occasion to take my girl away for the night and just chill without the kids," I said as I pulled her to me. "I just want you to relax and let me pamper you. You deserve it."

"Aaaawww, bae. That's so sweet. I'm about to cry." She sniffed.

A groan almost escaped, but I caught it in time. Her mood swings were all over the place. This pregnancy was worse than when she was pregnant with Keira. She went from zero to one hundred then cried after she got mad. I didn't understand it and didn't know what to do, but let her go through it.

"Nah, none of that. We making memories, remember? No crying."

She nodded her head with a sniffle. Then she walked over to the table and picked at the fruit tray. While she ate, I went into the bathroom and ran us some bath water. I sprinkled some of her vanilla bath salts in the water.

I went back into the room. Shaunie sat on the bed flipping channels. Grabbing her hand, I pulled her off the bed. "Let's go soak in the bath."

She stood up and followed me to the bathroom. "I can use a nice long soak. My back is killing me."

I undressed her, admired her body as I revealed inch by inch of her succulent skin. "Get in the water."

Watching as she eased in the water, I grabbed the washcloth and lathered it with soap. In past years, I didn't pamper her so. I used to massage her feet all the time, but I never really pampered her like this. When I was paralyzed, Shaunie did everything for me. She washed my ass and washed my hair. She kept me fed and took care of my kids. In my time of need, she remained steadfast in her love and devotion to me. Call me a pussy or whatever, but I had no problem getting on bended knee to wash her or take care of her in any capacity.

Shaunie leaned back in the tub. I washed her arms and legs. Instructing her to stand, I washed her private areas. "You want me to wash your hair?"

"No, I don't feel like being bothered with it."

"Alright. Dry off and come in the room. Imma get your night clothes out for you."

"Okay. I'll be right out."

I went to the drawer and pulled out her clothes. Earlier today, I came over and dropped off our overnight bags that I packed. Fishing through the contents, I pulled out her long maternity sleep t-shirt. After laying her clothes on the bed, I went to my suitcase and grabbed the box out of a compartment. Opening the box, I stared at the ring that nested inside. Plucking it out the velvet case, I fisted it in my hand. Once I was done, I walked over to the mini bar and poured me a shot of Hennessey. The liquor burned my throat as it went down. Thoughts raced through my mind. *What if she says no? Maybe it's too soon.* Doubts racked me, but I wasn't detoured from what I wanted. From what I needed.

Sitting on the sofa, glass in hand, is how she found me when she came out the bathroom. I had never seen a more beautiful sight than her, fresh from the tub with just a towel wrapped around her body. No make-up on her face. Just the natural glow of her beauty and her pregnancy.

Putting the glass down on the table, I beckoned her to me. "Come here." I held my arms open and spread my legs to make room for her to stand before me. Even sitting down, when she stood before me we were almost even. My head reached her chest. I wrapped my arms around her. Leaning down, I kissed her belly. Her hands sifted through my dreads. My passions stirred, but I ignored it. "Go put on your gown then come and sit by me."

I watched as she slipped the long sleep shirt over her head and put on her fuzzy socks. She turned to me and caught me staring. "What?" She walked over to me and sat down. "You sitting here looking all glum. What's wrong?"

"Nothing is wrong. Everything is just right." I opened my hand so she could see what I had. "The last time I asked you to be my wife, I did it all wrong. There was so many secrets I was keeping from you at the time. I should have never proposed knowing I wasn't being truthful to you." I paused to let her think about what I was saying. Tears pooled in her eyes. "This time I'm holding nothing back. Marry me. Let's make this official. I don't want to play house. I want to build a home with you and our kids."

Her hands covered her mouth. The tears, like diamonds, sat on her eyelashes. "What about the baby? What if the baby isn't yours?" she asked when she removed her hands.

I took her hands in mine. "It don't matter to me. Nothing matters to me, but you. I love you and want you to be my wife. Everything else is in the past. If the baby isn't mine, Imma still be his daddy because you are his mama. Tell me yes."

"Yes. I'll marry you."

I leaned over. My forehead touched hers. "I'm so glad you said yes. I was scared you wouldn't."

"There will not be a third proposal, Keyz. So do what you need to do."

"You can bet that. Never gotta sweat that," I said, saying the words from our song Sure Thing by Miguel. We hadn't listened to the song since she found out about my infidelities and child I had while with her.

Her breath tickled my lips before she began singing. "Even when the sky come falling."

"Even when the sun don't shine."

Simultaneously we sung, "I got faith in you and I."

I wiped the tears that trickled down her cheek. "So put your pretty little hand in mine. Even when we're down to the wire baby." My love for her was close to bursting. I loved her so much. It was sad that it took me this long and all the mistakes and fuck-ups I made to get to this point. But it was better late than not at all. I was glad she was still at my side after it was all said and done.

She placed a kiss to my lips. "Even when it's do or die."

"We can do it, baby, simple and plain, 'cause this love is a sure thing," we finished together.

Our love had been tested several times over the course of a year, but one thing I knew was we could get through anything, together.

***

Looking in the mirror, I inspected the fit of the custom made tux. A nigga was looking clean like an original mafia gangster, looking like I belonged on a GQ magazine. I didn't wear suits and tuxedos often, but when the occasion called for it, I went all out. This occasion definitely called for the best. In two weeks' time, Shaunie and I will be married. After proposing for the second time, we decided to have a speedy wedding before the baby arrived. I don't know about her, but I couldn't wait to put a ring on it and give her my last name.

"Fweeeeee." The sharp sound of a whistle pierced the air in the store. I turned around to see Thugga. "My nigga. You clean up nicely. Looking good in your monkey suit."

We dapped each other and gave a man hug. "Nigga, I know I'm on point, looking straight gangsta. Now you need to go try on your shit." I pointed to his suit. "I need all you niggas to have y'all tuxes fitted and ready. It's going down in a couple of weeks."

"I feel ya, big homie. Let me go in the back and put this here suit on," he said, grabbing the suit that was hanging up in the spot I indicated. "I hate that I have to wear this here tux. Imma outshine my man at his own wedding."

"You must have slipped and your nose landed in the product, because you must be high if you think that, my nigga."

He chuckled and walked to the back to go to the dressing room. Killer and Rayne arrived shortly after. We dapped each other before they grabbed their suits and headed to the dressing room. The tailor carefully pinned my cuffs and pants where I wanted them to be taken in.

My boys came from the back laughing and joking. "Man, these pants fit too damn tight. My nuts can't breathe," Killer said. He wore a grimace on his face as he pulled at the pants.

Playfully, Rayne pushed him. "They ain't tight. They are supposed to fit, dumbass." Killer hated to wear anything but sweatpants or jeans. Me and Thugga just shook our heads at them.

"Thugga, I know you ain't over there shaking your head. Nigga, your pants fit just fine because your ass ain't got no balls. Nikki carrying them bitches in her purse."

We burst out laughing at Killer's comeback. It was common knowledge in the group that Thugga was walking around like a love sick puppy since Nikki basically told him they were through for good. I felt bad for my homie. He did love her, this I knew. Many nights when we chilled over drinks, he told me how he felt about her. We didn't talk like bitches and go all in depth about our feelings. Thugga had a problem being with one woman, because he had something to prove. When he was much younger, he was molested by his mama's live-in boyfriend. He felt like his manhood was tested so he fucked a lot of bitches to prove to himself he was a man and he wasn't gay. In trying to prove something to himself, he may have lost someone he loved.

What a lot of people failed to realize was that everyone had a story. Some people's story was nicer than others. Some people's story affected their actions and shaped their lives forever, and not for the good.

"Man fuck y'all. I ain't worried about Nikki. She made her decision and it's cool." I heard the words as the lie it was. We all got quiet for a minute.

The tailor came back over to our section. He began fitting the suits one person at a time. Killer moaned and groaned the entire fitting.

Rayne turned to look at me from where he stood. "You ready for this man?" he asked me.

"Yeah, man. I been ready. That's my heart right there. She already mine. And I'm hers. We just getting the paper now to make it legal." I smiled.

He nodded his head. "I feel ya. My mom's and Pop's been together forever, you dig. That's commitment."

My palms started sweating and my breathing became shallow at the mention of forever. The word forever seemed like such a long time. Growing up, I had no examples of couples being fully committed to a relationship, let alone a marriage. Then my mind replayed all the times me and her had been together, happy and sad. Forever wasn't long enough, I realized. I wanted her this lifetime and the next. "I'm ready for that commitment," I told him.

On a lighter note, I thought about the surprise I had in store for Shaunie and the girls. My laughter was hard to contain. "But y'all check this out. Y'all know Shaunie 'n'em going out of town this weekend for her bachelorette party." When I had all of their attention, I ran down my surprise.

"Yo, that's wild as fuck," Thugga said.

"I want to be a fly on the wall." Thinking about what he said, Rayne shook his head. "Then again, no I don't."

Killer wore a smirk. "I ain't touching that one, my nigga. Y'all boys on your own with this one."

My surprise was going down in the history books. I just hope I don't go down in The Times Picayune newspaper obituary section.

Chapter 22

In friendships, you don't need to find the most interesting one. Just find the most loyal one.

-*Unknown*

Shaunie

"It just doesn't fit the way I envisioned," I cried with tears running down my face. Most of the tears were from just being hormonal, but the rest were just from wedding blues. We were at the bridal boutique for the dress fitting. When I got the dress last week, I loved it and thought it was perfect. Now I hated it. The material stretched across my stomach making me look like a whale.

"Mommy, why are you crying?" Keira asked me.

Looking down in my daughter's sweet face, I answered," I don't like my dress."

"But you look like a princess."

"Aaaawww, thank you, baby. I bet you are going to look like a princess too." I wanted to pick my baby up, but my stomach was getting too big and she was getting too heavy to carry in my condition. Keyz had expressly forbade me from holding anything past ten pounds. I mentally rolled my eyes at him. Ms. Lynn and my mom were here with us. I knew if I did try to pick her up, they would object and rat me out to him. They were straight old school when it came to pregnancy.

Stacy and Nikki stood next to me, holding my hand and rubbing my back. "The dress looks good, boo. Maybe we can get them to add just a little bit more material," Nikki said.

"Just calm down, Shaunie. We are going to get you the perfect dress, but you need to stop crying and calm down," Stacy said.

I took several calming breaths then nodded my head. For years, I dreamt of my wedding. Everything had to be perfect, at least in my mind. There wouldn't be another wedding for me. Like mother like daughter, when I say my marriage vows they are for eternity. The attendant came back to our section and handed me some Kleenex to wipe my face. "Thank you."

"No problem, sweetie. I see it all the time. Brides can get stressed out over the simplest of things, but that's okay. Who doesn't want their day to be perfect?" She placed her hand on my shoulder. "Now, we could add some extra material here." She pulled at the seams on the side of the dress. That would allow my stomach some room. "And take in some length in the front, but keep the back longer.

"That might work."

"Well, let's get it done."

I stepped back on the pedestal and looked in the mirror as she made adjustments. My face was puffy and my eyes were red from crying. This should be a happy moment, but I cried over something that wasn't really important. A fantasy played in my mind that when I went searching for my wedding dress I would find *the* dress. Being pregnant limited my choices, so I had to settle for a dress.

She stepped back when she was done. I didn't know if she was waiting for some type of approval or what, but she wasn't getting any from me. I was over this whole wedding debacle and just wanted to get this over with. I tried to step down from the pedestal, but had a little trouble. Nikki came forward, grabbed my hand to assist me.

"On the real, the dress is going to work, it doesn't look as bad as you think it does. Plus, there is no way to truly hide your six months pregnant belly."

"I'm not trying to hide it. I just don't want the dress to be all tight in that area, emphasizing it even more." I hated that I sounded like bridezilla. "Watch Keira until I change out the dress." I went inside the dressing room and quickly changed out of the dress and back into my clothes. I left the dress inside the dressing room, hanging up.

When I got back out, my mom and soon to be mother-in-law were standing on pedestals checking out their suits. Their cornflower blue skirt suits fit them amazingly. Sophisticated, yet sexy and appropriate. My color scheme for the wedding was cream, gold, and cornflower blue.

"Alright ladies. I'm loving those colors on y'all. It looks amazing."

Ms. Lynn cocked her hip to the side. "You already know. Me and ya mama gon' be on fleek." She high-fived my mom. These two together wasn't nothing nice. My mom was more conservative than Ms. Lynn, but she chilled all the way down when they got together.

"I love the suit. It highlights my curves perfectly," my mom said with a pretty blush on her face. I hadn't seen her blushing since before my dad died.

Teeth smacking from Ms. Lynn's direction, she said, "Uh huh, highlight them for Mike. Don't think I ain't notice y'all eyeballing each other at Keke's birthday party. Don't have me tell it."

My eyebrows hit my hairline. Mike and my mom? When did that happen? "What is she talking about?" I asked curiously. I wasn't mad or anything, just wanted to know. Hell, mama had a right to love too.

Playfully smacking her friend and my soon-to-be mom, she said, "Hush your mouth, Lynn, with that foolishness. Girl, don't listen to her. You already know she likes to play devils' advocate." She turned back to the mirror, making herself busy by looking at her skirt. "Mike and I just talked a few times on the phone, that's it."

"It's cool if it was more. I was just asking. Let me go check on my baby." I went to go check on Keira in the dressing room where Nikki took her to try on her dress. I ooohhh'd and aaahh'd over her dress then changed her back in her clothes. Keira's dress fit and she didn't need any further alterations. Stacy stood on the pedestal. Her dress needed altering because her slightly rounded stomach pulled too tight across her mid-section. She was still keeping the pregnancy a secret from Killer, but I didn't know how long that was going to last. Stacy was a little on the plump side and the thickness on her build helped to harbor the secret, but for how long, I knew not. It was only a matter of time before he took notice of the changes in her body when they got intimate or he saw her naked.

"I'm going to sit down while you go and try your dress on." I told Nikki. "Keira, come sit with me." She came over and sat on the bench with me.

The attendant came over and offered us some refreshments. I grabbed a bottle of water and chugged half of it down. My mom came and sat with us.

"I like your dress, honey," she said.

Shrugging my shoulder nonchalantly. "It's okay."

"Don't get the wedding confused with the actual marriage. A lot of people put more time and effort into the ceremony and not their marriage. Don't make the mistake of forgetting what's important. Even if you had to marry Keyon in rags, remember it's about the vows."

I thought carefully of what she said. In all reality, I would marry Keyz at the Justice of Peace if I had to. "You are right, mom. Thanks."

The rest of the crew came out. We grabbed the dresses and suits that were ready and arranged a date and time to pick up the rest. We decided to go and eat before me, Stacy, and Nikki had to meet up with a few of my other friends and cousins at the airport to fly out to Atlanta for my bachelorette party.

We went to the nearest restaurant. We talked and laughed about everything. Keira ignored the adults half of the time, opting to play with my phone. My mom and Ms. Lynn got along like childhood friends. With my mother's words about the marriage vows ringing in my ear, I pushed aside all my worries of the up-coming wedding and focused on what was important at the moment, spending time with my family.

***

The suite was filled with rambunctious noise from the crowd of women. It was me, Nikki, Stacy, Yuriah's wife Minnie, my cousin Dominque and a few other extended cousins and friends. They talked and laughed with glee as we waited for the male entertainers to arrive. Nikki and Stacy were able to secure the infamous male stripper RiDICKulous. I heard nothing but good, big things about his performance and couldn't wait to see for myself.

"Bay bae, I can't wait to see this mandingo," Nikki said, matching my sentiments.

"Oh yes, honey, he is everything I tell you. Lawd, the way that thing pops when he moves," Dominique said with a slight accent. She was my cousin on my mother's side of the family. We weren't close growing up, but recently linked up and started talking on the phone more. Atlanta was her stomping ground.

Lifting the glass of red wine, I took a sip. I had been sipping the same glass for the past few hours. The doctor gave me the okay me to drink red wine, but I didn't drink it frequently. Stacy followed suit with the wine and left the hard liquor to the other women who were drinking it like water. They were rowdy now, so I couldn't imagine the shenanigans that would take place once the male strippers arrived. "I hope so. I'm ready to do some bird watching."

The women laughed at my comment. We all were going to bird watch tonight. A knock on the door caused the women to cease talking. The room filled with silence. I remained in my chair as Nikki got up to answer the door. Everyone waited with bated breath to see who was at the door and for the fun to begin.

"What the hell?" Nikki exclaimed, not with excitement. She walked ahead of the men with a frown on her face.

I was confused until I saw a group of men come into the room. RiDICKulous was nowhere in sight. She told me she paid real good money to get him on such short notice. All the ladies were expecting him.

A tall, well-built white guy stepped forward from the group of men. The group consisted of men from several races, but all were sexy and handsome. "Where is the bride to be?" he asked.

I raised my hand. "That would be me."

"This is for you." He turned and nodded to his group. The men formed a straight line in the spacious suite. The leader of the group walked to the radio they brought with them. He pressed the button then went to get in line.

The excitement in the room raised another notch. I guess the women said strippers were strippers. They got their money ready to make it rain on them.

I leaned forward in my seat, a smile forming on my face. This was the highlight of the trip. The leader winked at me right before the music began to play. The sound of The Weather Girls' "It's Raining Men" poured out of the radio. At the same time, all the masculinity drained from the men to be replaced with femininity. My mouth dropped open in shock. Never in a million years would I have thought any of the men were gay. The way they moved their bodies and lip synced the song was undeniably homosexual.

"Oh My God." I turned to look at Nikki since she hired the entertainment. Her eyes were bugling out of her head.

"Oh, Lawd, save me. This is a sight for sore eyes," someone said with a groan.

Several other women stood shaking their heads. Many others put their money away and just stood with their hands on their hips. The men continued to dance and sing, even though they had to know that their presence was unwelcomed.

I stood up to whisper to Nikki and Stacy. "How in the fuck did this happen? No offense, but I'm sure no one here wants to watch dudes popping their dicks, especially since they play for the same team as us. This is a disaster."

"Hell, I ain't hire these motherfuckers. What the hell I look like getting gay men to dance for us?" Nikki snapped.

"Maybe it's some mix-up," Stacy said, ever the optimistic one.

By the end of the song, all the men were sporting erections from dry humping each other during their performance. Some of the women give dry applauses. The men noticed the women's reaction. They all wore smirks like they knew something we didn't.

"Thank you for the performance, though disturbing and unwanted as it was." I said being polite when I really wanted to tell them to get their shit and leave.

Nikki smacked her teeth. She walked over to the radio, picked it up, and handed it to the nearest man. "Here's your shit. Now get out." She didn't even try to hide her attitude. Several women nodded their heads in agreement. Someone even opened the door for them to leave. Still, the men didn't get offended.

"Hold on. Let me at least tip y'all for the trouble," I said.

The leader stepped forward. "The tip has already been taken care of." He smiled and walked away. The other men followed behind, exiting the room. Danielle, my other cousin, slammed the door behind them. She then went to the wet bar and drank Ciroc straight from the bottle.

"What the fuck was that?" my friend Keisha asked.

"Bitch, when you find out, let me know," Dominique said. "I almost passed out when they started rolling their dicks on the other's ass. What a waste of good dick."

We started talking and laughing at the shit that just went down in the room. No one could believe that the men were gay until we saw that dance. If we hadn't seen it with our own two eyes, we wouldn't have believed it at all. A person could walk pass one of the men on the street and would swear up and down he was straight.

Just then, my phone chirped, letting me know I had an incoming message. Keyz' name lit the screen. I slid the home screen to read the message.

Keyz: I hope you ladies enjoyed the stellar performance! #MaleStrippersAreOverratedAnyway #TheOnlyDickYoAssWillSee- IsMine #MakingMemories

He ended the message with a big ass smiley face emoji and a picture of him, Thugga, Killer, and Rayne laughing.

"That dirty dog." My outburst caused the women to look at me.

"What?" Danielle asked, still with the bottle in her hand.

I gave her my phone so she could read the message. "That's cold!" She passed the phone to the nearest person. My phone was passed around until everyone read the message. We all laughed. Now that the anger at not seeing who we came to see passed, we were free to laugh at the prank the men pulled on us.

"So, what we gon' do about it?" Nikki asked.

"What we are going to do is get our shit and hit the strip club, since our entertainment was ruined. Don't worry about the boys. I got something special planned for them." I grabbed my phone and purse.

The ladies started smiling and laughing at the idea of hitting the club. My mind was busy on payback. Two can play that game, but my game. I always play chess, not checkers. It's checkmate time. First thing in the morning, I was calling Wynter.

Chapter 23

Keep this in mind: Everyday give your all to your most loyal family and friends so at the end of the day, you can rest easy knowing that you have done your best to ensure their needs are met and well taken care of.

-Gebru Villars

Keyz

Wynter strutted into the private room at the Four Seasons. It was Thursday night and we got the club shut down for my bachelor party my crew threw me. I wasn't really feeling the stripper club scene since we come here to chill anyway. "Good evening, gentleman. Your entertainment will be in shortly." She smiled and winked at the fellows. Rayne groaned at her flirtatious behavior.

"Man, she works on my fucking nerve with that shit. Why her ass can't be like the other quads and chill. Fuck. They don't be with all the thirsty trap shit like her hot ass," he complained.

"Wyn does that shit to fuck with your silly ass. She probably laughs her ass off when she gets in back. You stay going ham for nothing," Killer said.

Yah! Bad bitches is the, Yah.
I ain't got no type.
Bad bitches is the only thing that I like.
You ain't got no life, nah.
Cups with the ice and we do this every night.
I ain't check the price, I got it.
I make my own money, so I spend it how I like.
I'm just living life.
And let my mama tell it I ain't living right.

"No Type" by Rae Sremmurd played over the speaker. The stripper walked into the room. My niggas let out catcalls and obscenities. I didn't know how she managed to make it in the room, because her heels were high as fuck. She had a black diamond studded bra on with a black diamond studded mini skirt that left little to the imagination. Her ass cheeks played peek-a-boo as she walked. She had long black hair that reached her ass. Her appearance was on point and her looks were enticing, but something about her seemed off to me. I forgot my discomfort when she started her performance.

She walked to the pole and spun around. Then she hopped on upside down. Her long hair trailed the floor. Dollars bills floated to the ground around her. Winding her hips to the beat, she reached behind her and pulled the strings to her bra. Slowly, she allowed it to fall to the ground, revealing pierced nipples.

"She fine as fuck," Man Man said, adjusting himself.

I leaned back with a blunt in my mouth and watched the show. It really didn't do shit for me, but my niggas was having a blast. Thugga stood watching, drinking on something. He seemed disinterested in the whole matter.

The stripper locked in on me and started walking my way. She placed her hands on my knees, but I moved them off me. I didn't want her to touch me or grind on me. I was done with that shit. Watching was all I would do. "No touching, ma."

She didn't say a word. She turned around and made her ass clap. I didn't so much as throw a nickel. Turning around to me, she licked her lips before flicking her tongue. I smirked at her antics. I done seen and heard it all when it came to females.

I thought I heard snickering, but shook my head. *I'm tripping*, I thought. She moved away from me and walked pass the men. Her hands caressed their chest and groped lower, but not grabbing their pieces.

Back at the pole, she ended her performance with a split.

The men clapped and whistled. She picked up her money before she walked back to me and handed me an envelope. Confused, I took it from her. She waited expectantly.

Hey baby. I hope Trinity was to your liking. Isn't she beautiful? Please tip her handsomely will you. Anyway, I love you. Shaunie.

A smile spread across my face. Shaunie sent me a stripper. Now that was something. I pulled a knot of money from my pocket and handed Trinity five one hundred dollar bills.

She reached for the money then stuff it in her bra. "Thank you," she said in a voice harder than mine, turning and walking out of the room. The rumble of her, his voice silenced the room and every nigga inside looked like he wanted to throw up. The bitch had the complete package to transfer him to a her, but the voice didn't lie. Niggas sported hard-ons for a shim, a she-male.

The stripper opened the door and there stood Nikki, Shaunie, Stacy, and Wynter. They were cracking up at us. They each wore smile that threatened to break their jaws they smiled so hard. "Enjoy the rest of your entertainment, boys. Sit back and relax. It's plenty more where that came from," Shaunie said, backing away from the door. I didn't attempt to go after her. I had every intention to punish that ass later tonight.

Payback was a bitch. A laugh erupted from my throat. My niggas looked at me like I had gone mad. Some threw me side eyes laced with disgust. "Shaunie n'em got us good for that lil' shit I pulled back in Atlanta."

"That's some fucked up shit she pulled, man. I ain't fucking with your girl no more," Man Man said before walking away, going to the other side of the room. He hardly hung out with me and my main crew. Man Man thought he was gon' get some pussy tonight. Shaunie's lil' treat ruined his plans. I just laughed at his ass.

Two security guards pushed their way in the door. A large five tier cake wheeled between them. They stopped in the middle of the floor then backed away. We all waited, cautious of our next surprise. "Did you order this?" I asked Thugga.

"No."

I looked to Rayne and Killer, they shook their heads no.

Finding my brother, Kamal, in the room, who stood next to Yuriah, I gave him a nod toward the cake, asking if they got it. They both shook their heads.

The song switched and 2 Live Crew's "Pop That Pussy" played. Suddenly, the top of the cake exploded and a woman popped out. Not just any woman, but a midget. All the niggas threw their heads back and groaned. Man Man gave me the finger. His young ass was disappointed like a muthafucka.

The midget tried to climb over the top of the cake, but her leg dangled over the edge, not touching the other tier. The bachelor party got turned into a comedy.

"I bet Nikki evil ass came up with this shit," Thugga said. I nodded my head in agreement. Shaunie wasn't this evil, or was she?

"Hey, I don't know, but Shaunie ass can go ham when she wants to," Rayne said, tossing back a drink.

Kamal walked over and grabbed the midget by her arms, helping her out of the cake she got stuck on. "You owe me," he mouthed to me.

I put my hand up with my fist balled to show him my tat that said "I am my brother's keeper." He put his up that matched the sentiment.

The woman danced around the men's legs, barely reaching their stomachs.

I grabbed the bottle of Ciroc and drunk straight from the bottle. If she had any more surprises in store beside this, we were in for a long night.

***

I pulled her hair and bit the back of her neck as I fucked her from behind. "You like this dick," I asked her as I deep stroked her. The juices from her body leaked on my thighs as I nailed into her repeatedly. I fucked her harder. Shaunie was gon' kill me.

"Yes. *Yes!* Fuck me just like that. That dick is so good, Keyz."

Not letting go of her hair, I pushed her head down. Making her ass toot up more. Wet slapping sounds echoed in the room. With my other hand, I smacked her ass hard, leaving my handprint on her flesh. "Take this dick. All of it." I shoved inside her. Passion had me in its grip.

She threw that ass back to me. Matching me stroke for stroke. "I'm cumming. Shit!" She released a long moan as her core tightened on me like a vice. I was so swollen and she was so tight, it bordered on pain.

My balls drew up and I came. "Aaaaahhhhh." Our mixed fluids ran on the sheets. Exhausted, I leaned on her back before placing a kiss to her shoulder blades. Slowly and carefully, I disengaged my dick from her body, already missing the warmth.

Shaunie turned to her side. I laid down next to her. *Wham!* She slapped my chest hard as fuck. "Didn't I tell you to stop pulling my damn hair that hard? That shit hurt. Felt like you was going to break my neck your grip was so tight."

I pulled her to me. "It ain't my fault your pussy that good I forgot. That shit was good, bae. I'm tired now. You done put me to sleep like a bitch."

"Shut up. Now you got my baby doing somersaults in here." She rubbed her belly. I placed my hand over hers.

"My baby know daddy was putting it down."

"Whatever. Go to sleep." She turned around and stuck her ass out. I turned and spooned her. My dick started to rise up again. "No. I'm tired." I didn't know why females thought it was okay to sleep with their ass out and a nigga was supposed to just lay next to them.

Grabbing my hard-on, I rubbed it on her ass. "Just let me put the head in."

She smacked her teeth. "Don't give me that just let me put the head in bullshit. You know your ass ain't gon' stop." I lifted her leg and slipped back inside, making her moan. I slowly pushed in and out. "This the last time."

I ignored her. We both knew we wasn't sleeping until I got my fill. I started pumping faster. I felt my nut building.

The shrill ringing of a phone broke my concentration. I tried ignoring the incessant ringing, but I couldn't. I started to remove myself from my girl, but she stopped me. "Don't answer. Keeping going, bae," she whined.

I tried to keep going, but the ringing was fucking with my mood. Slipping out of her, I reached for the phone on the night stand.

"You have a collect call from Terell Beauchamp," the operator said. I removed the phone from my ear and looked at it. *What the fuck Killer is calling me collect for"* "Press 1 if you accept the call."

I pressed one for my nigga. The operator put us through. Static filled the line for a second until his voice came though the line. "Keyz, I'm at OPP. Come bail me out."

"What they got you for?" I asked. I needed to determine if I needed to call my attorney before I headed to Orleans Parish Prison to get my main man.

"It's Stacy." He filled me in on what happened. My eyes sought out Shaunie. She sat up in bed with a puzzled expression on her face. I put my head down, chin touching my chest.

She took notice of my body language. "Keyz, what is it?"

I looked at her with pain-filled eyes. If it wasn't one thing it was another.

Chapter 24

Be loyal and trustworthy. Do not befriend anyone who is lower than you in this regard. When making a mistake, do not be afraid to correct it.

-Confucius

Shaunie

"Here Shaunie," Nikki said. I took the cup of tea she handed me that she got from the hospital cafeteria. Tentatively, I took a sip of the warm liquid. Immediately, it took the chill from me. When Keyz got the phone call a few hours ago from Killer, he told us that Stacy was in the hospital. She and Killer got into an argument after she told him about the baby. They started arguing about the baby not being his. Somewhere along the lines, Stacy fell down the stairs and Killer was arrested.

"Thanks, Nik. How you holding up?" We were in the waiting room expecting to hear word of Stacy's condition. Keyz dropped me off over an hour ago. He went to bail Killer out of jail. For what? No one knew exactly, but I knew it involved this incident because there was no way he wouldn't be here. As soon as I arrived, I was met in the room by Stacy's mother, father, and a few of her relatives. Her mother told me what Stacy was able to tell the EMS workers had happened before she lost consciousness.

Nikki leaned her head back and stared at the ceiling. "About the same as you. That's my fucking friend back there. I swear if it isn't one thing it's another. A little over a year ago, we sat in these very chairs after Thugga and Keyz was in that shoot-out. Since that night, everything just seemed to go downhill."

Nodding my head in understanding, I was tired of coming to the hospital. It seemed like we stayed up here over one of our loved ones. We had been blessed that we hadn't lost anyone. "It does seem like that. If anyone would have told me a year ago Keyz and I would have separated then got back together after I started feeling someone else, then getting kidnapped, watching my ex-lover get killed by his brother, the love of my life getting shot then paralyzed by said brother, being pregnant and not sure of my child's father, having custody of my man's secret child, my best friend and her man breaking up for good, Keyz finding out he had a brother, and now Stacy being pregnant and in the hospital, I wouldn't have believed a word." My head hurt from keeping up with all the bad shit that had gone down in a year's time.

"You ain't never lied." She huffed. "I thought me and Thugga would stand the test of time. It was us against the world, you know. Now, I struggle every day with the decision to leave. In spite of the struggle it's the best decision I have ever made. I have no worries over if he is going to come home or if he fucking another bitch. I have peace. And let me tell you, ain't nothing like it."

"I hear ya. I wish we had some peace and didn't have to run up to anymore hospitals."

I leaned my head on her shoulders and she leaned her head on my head, taking comfort from each other. I don't know how long we stayed like that. My phone chirped, alerting me to an incoming message. Lifting my phone, I saw Keyz' name on the home screen. Swiping my finger, I read the message.

Keyz: What's up bae?

I sent him a text back.

Me: We are just waiting on word about Stacy.

Immediately he texted back.

Keyz: I'm sure everything is cool. She gon' pull through. I'm waiting for them to let Killer out so I can get some info on what the fuck went down.

Shaunie: I want to know what went down too. This shit is crazy. We were all just chilling and laughing over our bachelor and bachelorette parties. Now Stacy laid up in a hospital bed suffering from Gods knows what and Killer locked up over some bullshit.

Keyz: For real. That nigga should be coming out any minute. Wainwright done got everything handled. We gon' be there as soon as he is released.

Shaunie: Okay. I'll see you in a lil' bit.

Keyz: You need something before I come?

Shaunie: No bae. I'm good.

Keyz: I love you.

The sentiment from him never ceased to make me smile.

Shaunie: Love you too.

With a smile on my face, I put my phone away. The waiting room was quiet. With sober faces, everyone waited on pins and needles. Stacy's parents sat in the chairs across and down from us. Her mom stared straight ahead. Her father rubbed his wife's back soothingly.

I turned to Nikki to see her browsing through her phone. Leaning over, I saw that she was looking at pictures. Nothing but happy times showed on the pictures. They illustrated me, her, and Stacy at my bachelorette party, Keira's birthday, and several older pictures.

"Girl, I remember those times like yesterday," I told Nikki.

"Me too. These picture captured those blessed moments I had with y'all. I love y'all. My sisters for life."

We hugged each other tight. Held on for dear life. After several heartbeats, we broke apart. Wiping away the tears we shed, we looked at more pictures. Some made us cry, many made us laugh.

Our laughter caused Stacy's family to look over at us questioningly. I passed them the phone to look at our pictures from years ago. The pictures broke the strain in the room. Just seeing happier times lifted spirits. We all got lost in the past, in the memories.

But past memories had no chance against the here and now, reality. A doctor came into the waiting room. Cleaning his throat, he asked for the family of Stacy Wallace. Nikki and I got up and followed her parents to where the doctor stood.

He motioned us away from the crowd so that he could tell us about Stacy's condition privately. "Mr. and Mrs. Wallace, as you know, Stacy fell down the stairs. In the fall she sustained an injury to the head. Often times with head injuries, symptoms can be delayed. She was conscious for a short while after the fall, but soon experienced slurred speech, blurred vision, and nausea. This led us to believe she suffered a concussion. At the time of her arrival here, she was unconscious. Further examination revealed she has bleeding on the brain which in turn caused swelling. The bleeding and swelling increased the pressure on the brain tissue. The team of physicians decided surgery was the best option to alleviate swelling."

"Yeah. Yeah. We know all this. Tell me how my baby is doing right now," Stacy's mom, Yolanda, said.

"Now, honey. Calm down and let the doctor tell us what he needs to."

Nikki and I stood quietly.

The doctor continued. "During surgery we discovered significant bleeding in the brain. We did the best we could. At this time, she is unresponsive. We put her on a respirator to assist with breathing. The baby is fine, at the moment, but that can change."

Ms. Yolanda released a sob. Mr. Ronnie pulled her into his arms. My hand sought Nikki's. I gave her hand a squeeze. The doctor stood before us with an unreadable expression on his face. In this line of business, it was best to shield your emotions, since this job required a person to give bad news to families on a daily basis.

"When can we see her?" Ms. Yolanda asked

"She's in recovery right now. Give or take a few hours."

"What happens now?" I asked.

"Now, we pray for the best. I'm sorry." He said as he walked away, leaving us to grieve. The possibility that we could lose Stacy was very real.

Mr. Wallace carried his wife over to the chair. The rest of the family flocked to them. They offered well wishes and some prayed.

Me and Nikki huddled together, grabbing each other tight. We prayed that our clique of three wasn't reduced forever to a clique of two. Stacy and I had plans to raise our babies together. This wasn't how it was supposed to be. An argument led to an accident, in turn leaving my friend, my sister, fighting for her life. The baby growing inside her, the one she had wanted for so long, may never take a breath. "Lord Jesus, please please don't take my friend away from me. It can't be her time yet," I prayed aloud. This couldn't be happening. There was no way life could be this cruel. In the mist of my happiness, two days before by wedding where Stacy was supposed to walk down the aisle as my bridesmaid, we were yet again in a hospital.

Chapter 25

Everybody wants loyalty, consistency, and somebody who won't quit. But everybody forgets that to get that person, you have to be that person.

-Ritu Ghatourey

Keyz

"Man, them muthafuckas taking long as fuck to release my nigga," Thugga proclaimed as he leaned against the building smoking a cigarette.

We stood outside of Central Lockup waiting for Killer to be released. It was late Friday night, close to early Saturday morning. The people in the city must have been acting up for the weekend because since waiting, NOPD squad cars had been arriving every fifteen to twenty minutes with sometimes two and three people in the back of the cars. Several hours earlier I got a phone call from Killer telling me he got locked up after fighting with Stacy. "Wainwright got him processed hours ago, but you know them miserable bitches that work up in here is taking their fucking time."

I paced back and forth on the sidewalk across the street from the jail. With the way NOPD be looking to jack niggas up, I didn't need them looking my way for shit. They thought a black man wearing dreads and jeans was always suspicious of a crime. Pulling my phone from my pocket, I looked at my screen for messages from Shaunie. On top of worrying about my round getting locked up, my girl's best friend was laid up in the hospital being operated on. Not seeing any messages, I sent Shaunie a quick text to let her know where I was so she wouldn't worry. She was 7 months pregnant, she didn't need anything else to be concerned over.

"Yo, there that nigga go now." Thugga patted my arm to get my attention. "Over here," he yelled out.

179

Killer looked over in our direction. Noticing us, he jogged across the street. Putting my phone back in my pocket, I held out my hand for a dap. "What up." He dapped my hand and went in for a man hug, but I pushed him back. "Nah dawg. Niggas go to jail then they come out twerking and shit. We keeping nothing but space between us," I chuckled, fucking with him.

Thugga started cracking up.

"Fuck you niggas. Ain't shit gay 'bout me. Ask ya mamas." He pounded my fist then turned and pounded Thugga's. "Man, let's get the fuck from around here. Ten feet from lock up ain't enough room for me." He looked back at the jail with disgust.

"I feel ya." I told him as I turned in the direction of Tulane Ave. "We going to the hospital, right?"

We walked up the street where I parked my car. Killer told us who he saw in jail, but ignored my question about going to the hospital. Quickly, I looked over at Thugga. We looked at each other with a question in our eyes. *What's going on with them?* I thought. Deciding to save my questions for the confines of the car, I dropped the question.

Making it to the car, I pushed the key fob to unlock the doors. Thugga rode shot gun and Killer took the back. I pulled out and merged into traffic. Even though it was early morning hours Tulane Avenue stayed busy. Turning down the radio, I looked in the rearview mirror and caught Killer's eye. "What the fuck happened with you and Stacy?"

"For real. Y'all motherfuckers hardly ever fight. Fuck you get locked up for?" Thugga said when he took a second to stop rolling a blunt.

Killer sighed before he spoke. "Them motherfuckers arrested me for battery against a police officer and resisting arrest. I punched one of them bitches in the face when he tried to stop me from getting in the ambulance with Stacy's hoe ass. I'm mad at the bitch, but I hope she alright." Hearing him speak of Stacy like that shocked the hell out of me. He never talked about her that way.

"Why she a hoe?" Thugga asked, taking the words out of my mouth.

"This bitch talking about she pregnant," he said angrily.

The car got quiet. No one said a word as we absorbed what he said. We knew what was troubling Killer now. Thugga lit the blunt once he was done rolling it. He took a hit of the weed. I was about to jump to his side until something told me to get him to talk. Treading carefully, I spoke. "And you think it ain't yours." It was a statement not a question.

"Think! Nigga, I know it ain't mine. She been talking that baby shit, so I started using condoms and I watch her ass take birth control pills every morning."

"Man, you doing all that instead of just telling her the truth," I shook my head.

He put his head down and shook his head. "I can't tell her. How you admit to your girl you are less than a man? I couldn't do it."

Thugga passed the weed to Killer. "Man, I would raw dog the shit out of Nikki if I knew she wouldn't get pregnant."

Killer took the weed and hit it. "Nigga, Nikki wouldn't let you eat her pussy let along hit it. And, you ain't the one who is sterile."

"May be sterile," I interjected.

When Killer was a kid, he was diagnosed with mumps. His mama was a young, single mother and didn't keep up with his vaccinations like she should have, leaving Killer prone to get every childhood disease imaginable with mumps being the more serious.

"All the bitches I done fucked ain't get pregnant. Her ass been out here cheating." His tone and body language conveyed that he was convinced that she was cheating and there was no possibility that the baby Stacy carried could be his.

"Them bitches you done fucked probably was on the shot or aborted your seed or some shit. You can't go off that. Plus, you know your ass was fucking nothing with no rubber anyway. Ya mama said the doctor said there was a small chance that fertility could return." I drove to the hospital. Killer was mad now, but he needed to be there for Stacy. This could all turn out to be a big misunderstanding and he would have regrets.

He looked up at me with a hopeful expression. "You think it could be mine?" I felt like I hadn't been a decent friend to my dawg. Having my own issues and problems, I never took the time to realize how he might have felt about not being able to father a child. He was a damn good uncle to my kids and Lil' Thugga.

"Anything is possible," I said.

He nodded his head. "Take me to the hospital."

"I was already going there. But you still never said how she ended up in the hospital though."

"When she told me she was pregnant, I slapped the shit out of her and denied it was mine. She cried and begged for me to listen to her, but I wasn't trying to hear shit. I was leaving the house. She followed me out the bedroom and was pulling and grabbing on my shirt to keep me at the house. I jerked away from her and she lost her grip." He paused as he replayed the scene in his mind. "She fell down the stairs when she lost her grip. We were arguing right by the staircase."

"Damn, man. That's some crazy shit. Weird ass accident," Thugga said.

"I know right. Man, I called the ambulance, 'cause she was slurring and shit. Why when the medics and the cops got there them bitches was trying to get me for domestic violence until Stacy spoke up against that shit."

"Boy, your ass lucky she was conscious enough to tell them. With her in the hospital, your ass would have been looking at attempted murder or some shit like that. They would have thrown the book at you," I said.

"For real," Killer said. He leaned back with the blunt between his lips.

The rest of the ride to the hospital was quiet with the exception of the radio playing in the background. We smoked the blunt to help us chill from the stress of the events of the last twenty-four hours.

When we made it to the hospital, I parked my car then sent Shaunie a message to let her know we were outside in the parking garage and on our way up. She sent a message back letting me know which waiting room they were in.

We walked inside, but made a detour to the cafeteria to get the girls something to eat and drink. They had been here for several hours waiting on word about Stacy's condition. Killer decided to grab coffee for Stacy's mom and pop.

Loaded down with food and drinks, we made our way to the waiting room.

I headed straight to my girl. She stood up when she saw me walking her way, her hands rubbing her back. I took a moment to study her. She had circles under her eyes from not getting any sleep the night before. But to me, she looked beautiful. Not just her looks, but her inner beauty. She possessed a quiet strength that many people confused with weakness.

"Hey, bae." She placed her hands on my shoulder and leaned in to kiss me. Her petal soft lips touched mine. It was a quick peck, but it lasted long enough for me to feel her love for me.

Balancing her drink and food in one hand, I snaked my arm around her waist to pull her close. "How you feeling?"

"I'm just tired."

I kissed her forehead then handed her the hot tea and sandwich. "Sit down and eat your food."

She grabbed her tea and sat down. I sat next to her. I watched as Thugga hesitantly walked over to Nikki who sat four chairs over from where me and Shaunie sat. Thugga looked nervous as he approached her. He said something to her that I didn't hear before he offered her a drink and the food he got especially for her. She looked like she wanted to turn him down, but she reluctantly took his offering and gave him a small smile. He sat next to her and she turned to him with a frown.

"The doctor said Stacy has swelling on the brain. The surgery was as successful as it could be. Now we're just waiting to see if she improves."

I looked at her incredulously because I had no idea her condition was that serious. "I don't think Killer knows it's that bad. I gotta go tell him," I said getting up to catch up to him. He was making his way over to Stacy's parents.

Just as I was getting up, he approached Stacy's parents and all hell broke loose.

Chapter 26

A real friend is someone that will be there for you, and expect nothing in return but your love and loyalty. Real friends know that you aren't perfect and don't ask you to be. All a real friend will ask you for is to be a real friend back when they need one.

-Keren Zhims

Shaunie

It was pandemonium inside the waiting room as Thugga grabbed Killer away from Stacy's family when he approached them. One minute me and Keyz was talking. The next minute, Stacy's mother knocked the coffee from Killer's hand when he approached them.

The liquid splashed on Killer's arm. It had to have been hot because they just got it from downstairs, but he didn't respond when the hot coffee touched his arm, surely burning it. Some of Stacy's relatives stood up to intervene, but stopped when Mr. Ronnie grabbed Ms. Yolanda.

I stood up, but Keyz pushed me behind him. He glanced away from the scene to look at me. The look he gave me froze me in my spot. He didn't need to say the words "keep your ass right where you are" for me to understand what he was saying. I knew not to go against him when he was in protective mode.

Stacy's dad held Ms. Yolanda back. "You got some fucking nerve showing up here. Then you have the audacity to offer me some damn coffee. Fuck you and your coffee. My baby wouldn't be laid up in this damn place if it wasn't for you."

Killer's facial expression didn't change, but his body language and slumped shoulders, conveyed the guilt he was feeling.

"Yolanda! That's enough. You are causing a scene. Stacy told the EMS medics that he didn't push her. You are falsely accusing this man," Mr. Ronnie tried to reason with her, but there was no reasoning with a grieving mother.

The rest of the family stood by, but didn't say anything. They didn't appear to have any animosity toward Killer. I stood behind Keyz, my protective shield, in case something popped off. My rounded stomach brushed his back. With bated breath, I waited for Ms. Yolanda to calm down.

"Enough my ass!" My eyes widened in shock to hear her talk to her husband that way. In all the time I had been around them, they never so much as raised their voices toward each other. "It's his fault. Stacy told me weeks ago she was pregnant and afraid to tell you because you didn't want no kids. I bet that's what this argument that landed her here was about."

In shame, he put his head down, because it was indeed the reason why. Seeing how she was making him feel, Ms. Yolanda went in on Killer.

"That's right. What type of nigga are you to deny your baby? My daughter ain't been nothing but good to you. She don't deserve this shit." She broke down crying at the end.

Mr. Ronnie led her away to the opposite end of the waiting room. While walking away, Killer called out to them.

"I'm sorry. It was an accident. I would trade places with her in a heartbeat." He turned and walked away. Thugga nor Keyz went after him. He needed time only with his thoughts.

Just like NOPD, the hospital security came after the incident was done and over. Nikki walked over and talked to them. Satisfied with the resolution, they walked away. We waited a few more hours to hear any update on her condition. I laid my head on Keyz' shoulder. He tried to convince me to go home and rest since there wasn't anything that could be done. I just didn't feel right leaving until I knew my best friend was going to be okay. Close to noon, my back began to hurt from sitting in the uncomfortable chair. I decided I was going to go home for a few hours to rest then come back.

I turned to Keyz. "Bae, I think I need to go home for a few hours. My back is killing me."

He stood up and grabbed my hand, helping me up. "You can't be stressing out the baby."

He entwined our hands as we walked toward Stacy's parent to let them know I was leaving for a few. We were several feet away from her parents when the doctor from earlier came walking into the waiting room with a solemn expression of his tired face. He walked directly toward us. My heart started beating faster. I knew what he was going to say before he said it. I squeezed Keyz' hand. My steps slowed. He turned to look at me questioningly. My eyes stayed on the doctor as he made it to Stacy's parents before us. He followed the direction of my eyes.

Stacy's parents stood up when the doctor stood before them. He motioned with his hands for them to follow him. I watched as they stepped away from the crowd and walked to the hall. After several heartbeats, a loud wail was heard from the hall.

My eyes closed as pain consumed me. Unchecked, tears flowed down my cheeks. Keyz held me in his arms, but in that moment his arms weren't enough. My best friend, who was like a sister to me, was gone.

Cries broke out around us. I opened my eyes and I noticed two things. One, Mr. Ronnie literally was carrying Ms. Yolanda in his arms as she broke down screaming and yelling for Stacy. Her anguish resonated in my soul. Two, the hospital clock's bold red numbers. At 11:59 a.m., Stacy Wallace and her unborn baby died.

***

It's been three weeks since Stacy died. The funeral and second line, New Orleans traditional brass band parade, was a blur in my mind. The details of her home-going was hazy at best. I remember being present, but it seemed like an out of body experience. Who thinks of burying their twenty-five year old friend? Nikki and I talked everyday just to check on each other, but I spent most of my time at home with the kids. Going around town was hard to do, because everything I did was a constant reminder of my friend. I was still in a state of shock. Not believing she was really gone, I called her cell phone hoping she would pick up. Instead of her answering, I got the voicemail. Hearing her voice on the recording did nothing to soothe my soul.

Lying in bed, my hand traveled to my stomach to caress where my baby rested. Stacy and I had so many plans with our new babies. It wasn't every day that best friends carry at the same time. A tear fell from my eyes, but I quickly brushed it away. Happy thoughts are what I needed to think of. My baby's health depended on me staying calm.

"What are you over there thinking about?" Keyz' voice shook me from my thoughts. He hadn't left my side from the time we left the hospital after the doctor informed us of her passing. "I'm thinking about Stacy." There were no emotions behind my words, just deadpan.

He pulled me closer and kissed my head. "I'm so sorry, bae. I still can't believe it." His hands rubbed up and down my arms. "You got to try to stay calm for the baby."

I nodded my head. Being in the room all day wasn't going to change the fact that my friend was dead. I still had to live for my family. "You're right. Let's get the kids out the house. Maybe we can go for a ride on the lake." I stood up to go and put on some clothes.

Wham! His hand slapped me hard on my ass. "That's my girl."

I turned around and punched him in the chest. "That shit hurts. Stupid ass."

He forcefully grabbed my arms, pulling me to him. "Let me kiss it." He licked his lip. Usually that would get me in the mood, but today wasn't one of those days.

Pouting, I shook my head before putting my head on his chest.

Keyz grabbed my face, forcing me to look at him. His strong hands captured my head. "Everything is going to be okay. I know it doesn't seem like it right now, but I promise it will. I love you."

"I love you. I know it's going to take a minute, but it will get better." We rested our forehead on each other's and I took what comfort I could from him.

Nikki Tee

Chapter 27

Loyalty, honesty, and friendship are hard to come by. It's uncondi-
tional, it's heartfelt, and it's always being honest with those who
matter the most.

-Nishan Panwar

Keyz

Hunched over my desk at the car wash, I poured over paperwork
that required my attention. Over the past six weeks, I had been
mostly home tending to my kids and Shaunie. Now, I was playing
catch up at work until my meeting with Thugga, Killer, and Rayne
started.

A knock at the door snagged my attention. Looking up, Thugga
walked through the door with his usual carefree swag.

"What's up," he said as he breezed in the room and walked directly to the mini refrigerator. Taking a cold drink, he sat across
from me.

"Nothing, man. Trying to get caught up on all my work and
maybe get ahead. Shaunie gon' be dropping the baby soon. I ain't
gon' have time to be coming over here or going to the other business
for a lil' minute. That's one of the things I need to holla' at y'all
about."

He took a swig of the Coke before responding. "You already
know we got you. Just tell us what you need. Hell, I signed and paid
all the invoices to your businesses after you got shot and was down
for the count. It ain't nothing for me to handle that. Rayne kept the
payroll going and Killer kept the employees in line." He paused and
looked thoughtful for a second. "Though I'm thinking Killer ain't
gon' be much help right about now. He got a lot going on. Ya feel
me?"

Killer was on a downward spiral. After the doctors pronounced Stacy's death, he got a DNA test done on the fetus. The baby boy that she carried was indeed Killer's baby. He took her death hard, but after finding out that the baby was his, he seemed to lose it. Guilt consumed him over their untimely deaths. He spent most of his time drinking and smoking. Business took a back burner. I understand his pain and loss too well.

"Yeah, bruh, I know. He taking it hard. It's gon' be a while for him to recover from that."

"How Shaunie holding up?"

"She holding up okay. The kids keep her busy. And she's mindful of the load she carrying. All that crying was making her sick and distressing the baby. I ain't letting her wallow in her pain though. What about Nikki?"

He looked away with a sigh. Ever so slightly, his shoulders hunched. I thought him and Nikki was getting closer since Stacy's death. Shaunie told me he had spent a few nights over at the house. I didn't ask him about it, because that was his business. Having someone close to you die usually makes people seek comfort in the familiar, but his body language spoke differently. "She was messed up the first few weeks or so. I stayed at her house to help with Lil' Thugga. Last I checked she was back at work. She sounded good. I haven't talked to her in a week. She ain't answering my calls anymore."

"Shaunie hasn't mentioned anything, but I'm sure she's good."

"Oh, I know she good. She dropped my son off at my mama's house yesterday for me to pick up. She just ain't trying to fuck with me."

"What happened with y'all crazy muthafuckas now?" I leaned back and rubbed my growing beard.

He put his head down and ran his hands through his dreads before looking back up. "That's just it. Ain't shit happen. I tried telling her I'm through with all that fucking around with hoes and shit. I

192

asked her if I could come back home. When I stayed with her those few days, I was in the house by nightfall. I even left my phone on the counter so she had access to it. No passcode or nothing. She ain't trying to hear shit. I don't know what else to do. She said she ain't fucking with me on no level."

The depression in his voice could be heard. I could definitely relate to him. When Shaunie left me, I felt empty. Everything I worked for and the risks I took in the streets wasn't worth being without that one woman who had my back regardless of what I had to offer.

"How you feeling about that though?" I asked, trying to see where his mind was at.

"Nigga, how you think? I ain't gon' pretend I ain't fucked up about it. I miss my girl. My family. The whole time we was together I was out here fucking around smashing different bitches. We ain't even together right now and I'm out here faithful as fuck. I ain't fuck nothing, but my palm in months. My son living under a different roof than me. My girl going on dates with square ass niggas and I can't say or do shit about it. What right do I have? I fucked up."

I nodded my head in understanding. Sitting on the sideline while the woman you love date other men wasn't pleasant. Men often dished it out, but we couldn't take it.

"I feel ya. Just give her more time. Keep your head on straight."

A knock at the door interrupted us. We stopped talking and waited for the person knocking to come through. The door was pushed open and Rayne came into view. No sooner than Rayne came over the threshold, Killer followed behind. I smelled him before I saw him. The strong odor of alcohol seemed to follow behind him, just like the cloud of despair clung to him.

He staggered to the chair without speaking to anyone. Plopping down, he sagged in the chair and leaned back. We all got quiet as we took in his appearance. He face was ashen. He eyes had dark circles around them like he hadn't slept in days. He wore sweat pants and a t-shirt with tennis shoes. The nights of drinking and smoking was taking a toll on him.

Grief consumed him. In turn, he constantly consumed alcohol to chase away the pain and guilt. It was barely noon and he was close to drunk. I knew he was grieving, but it didn't sit right with me that he was falling apart like this.

"Killer, my nigga, what's up with you?"

Barely holding up his head, he looked at me. "Man, nothing. Been chasing this paper. Trying to keep it moving," he slurred drunkenly.

I knew it was a lie. The only thing he had been chasing was the bottle and his demons. Deciding not to let it slide, I spoke up. I couldn't stand by and watch my dawg destroy himself. "Listen man, I can't pretend to understand what you are going through. I know it's hard, but you gotta get it together. Stacy wouldn't want you to carry on like this."

Out of nowhere, Killer took on a defensive posture. "You right you don't know what the fuck I'm dealing with. I said I'm cool. Get off my dick."

I held my hands up in surrender. The way my mindset was set up, I wanted to knock his ass out for being disrespectful toward me. My temper was short-circuited and it hardly needed any nudging to go off. However, I rubbed the bridge of my nose to calm myself down. In the heat of the moment, things are said and done that normally wouldn't if both parties stayed calmed and rational.

Ever the peacemaker in the crew, Rayne leaned forward in his chair and turned his body slightly so he was facing Killer. "Yo, ain't nobody trying to check you, Killer. Yous our boy and we just trying to look out for you."

"I appreciate it, but I'm good."

He said he was good so I left it at that. He was my dawg and I had mad love for him, but I couldn't make a grown man get himself together. The silence stretched for a few seconds until I cleared my throat and got down to the business at hand. The whole while we discussed business I couldn't ignore the nagging feeling that came over me.

***

It was after 9pm on a Saturday. Me, Shaunie, and the kids were on I-10 going home after seeing the kids movie Inside Out. Traffic on the high-rise was at a standstill and backed up for several miles. Flashing lights could be seen up ahead. With the way the cars were honking and blowing their horns, I'm surprised Keira and Shaun could stay asleep in the back seat.

"Bae, I hope we hurry and get through. I gotta pee bad." This pregnancy had her getting up through the night peeing every two to three hours.

I didn't think we were getting through no time soon. On a normal day traffic on the high-ride was crazy. Add an accident in the mix and it was a disaster. "You might have to cop a squat on the shoulder. These rubbernecking muthafuckas got traffic backed up."

"I ain't pissing outside or in public. Besides, you get a stye on the eye."

I wanted to laugh at how superstition she was. "Well, you better grab one of Keira's back-up pull-ups and slap it on your ass." Even though my baby girl was potty-trained, we kept back-up pull-ups in the car in case we had to take long trips and she couldn't hold it in.

She mushed my head playfully. "Stop making fun of me." She folded her arms over her chest and pouted her lips.

"Give me some kisses." I puckered my lips and leaned over the console.

Her soft lips touched mine and I forgot we were in traffic as I got lost in the feelings she invoked in me.

The blaring horn broke us apart. Finally, traffic moved at a snail's pace when an officer started directing it. Up ahead, I saw the flashing lights of the police cruisers and the ambulance. A car had slammed head first against a guardrail.

"Bae, that looks like Killer's car," Shaunie said, leaning forward in her seat to get a better look.

Slowing down, I looked over at the car. It did look like my dawg's car, but I couldn't see the license plate. "Killer is probably at the Four Seasons chilling."

We got closer to the car. The windshield looked as if someone flew through it. Officers stood around something on the ground. I wasn't sure, but it looked like a sheet-covered body. I couldn't see the license plate because the trunk was facing the opposite way. The cars behind me got impatient at the pace of the movement. The other drivers were rubbernecking trying to see what was happening. I was looking for a different reason.

My palms got sweaty the closer we got. My stomach muscles tightened. I kept telling myself that it wasn't his car. But in the back of my mind I knew it was possible. Especially with all the drinking he had been doing lately. After our sit down last week, he seemed to be getting better.

I got right up on the car and almost stopped to get a look at the plate. KILLA1 it read.

"Baby, that's his car!" Shaunie yelled.

Cars behind us blew their horns, demanding for us to move. I drove forward, but switched lanes to get on the shoulder. I threw open the door and ran across the lanes to get to where the officers were standing.

The officers turned when they heard me coming. One of them held his hand out to stop me.

"You can't be over here. This is a scene."

I heard him, but my eyes stayed glued on the body. My gut told me it was my round, my friend. "That's my friend's car," I choked out, pointing at Killer's black BMW. "Is that him?" I couldn't imagine anybody else having his car.

"Sir, I understand that you are upset, but we can't let you go near the body."

I felt my pain manifesting into anger. One of the officers must have noticed how I was struggling to contain myself. He took pity on me because he came over with an ID in his hand.

"This isn't the normal procedure, but I can understand your pain. Here is the identification card that was found on the victim," he said as he handed me the card to look at it.

I grabbed the card from his hand. Turning it over, I looked at the picture. The familiar face of my friend stared back at me. I couldn't do anything but stare back. Sadness, pain, and guilt racked me. Maybe I should have tried harder to get through to him when I saw he was struggling with dealing with losing Stacy and the baby.

Nodding my head, I gave the sympathetic officer back the card. I looked at my dawg's body before I walked away. In a daze, I walked back to the car. I was silent when I got back in.

Shaunie put her hand over her mouth and covered up a sob. I stared straight ahead. "I'm so sorry, baby."

She leaned over the console and hugged me. I placed my head on her shoulder and took comfort from her. In less than two months' time, we both buried one of our best friends. I felt raw with emotions, shock and disbelief that he was gone. I just spoke with him the other day. The numbness coursing through me made it hard for me to feel any sort of sadness. It seemed unreal.

Nikki Tee

Chapter 28

To find love in all the right places, one must look for loyalty, under-standing, respect, peace, unconditional love. To look into someone's eyes you see one's soul.

-Unknown

Shaunie

"Yaaaaassss, bae! Just like that." I was throwing my ass to Keyz as he hit it from behind. My tunnel was dripping wet. Face down, ass up was the position he had me in. It was the only position we could have sex in. I was due in two weeks, but that didn't stop us from going at it like rabbits. The closer I got to my delivery date, the more I wanted some dick. My hormones were crazy.

Grabbing a hold of my hips, Keyz rotated his hips in a circular motion, causing him to hit my G spot and I moaned into the pillow. "You like that, huh?" He rammed me a little too hard. It felt like he was hitting my damn cervix.

I put my hand on his stomach, trying to restrict how deep he could go. "Shit. That was too deep."

Leaning over, he kissed me. His tongue caressed the crease of my lips, demanding entry. I allowed him and he devoured me. He kissed me so passionately I had no choice but to respond back. I was so into the kiss, I forgot about the slight sting of pain I felt.

"Take this dick. It's yo dick," he whispered in my ear. His tongue snaked out and licked the inside of my ear.

His words were such a turn on to me. My core clenched and tightened before a puddle leaked from me. "Yes." He had me panting like I ran a race.

He sat back up and got to work. All I could do was take the dick. He was relentless in his strokes. My elbows could no longer support me, so I dropped down to my face.

"Ah, fuck bae! This pussy so damn good."

I held on to the covers as he dug all up in me. It felt like he was trying to fuck my baby out of me. No lying though, it hurt so damn good. My inner muscles kept clenching like a vice.

He pulled out of me and slapped my ass with his thick anaconda that was slicked with my juices. He nudged my anus with his head.

"Don't you fucking dare," I hissed with so much venom his ass paused. I wasn't down with no anal. We tried it once and I cried like a bitch for him to take it out. Any man who had over eight inches of dick didn't have any business trying to fuck anybody in the ass.

He chuckled as he rubbed it up and down my slit back to my ass. "Damn, bae, chill. I wasn't gon' put it in." He continued to rub. "I was getting ready to nut and I ain't want to."

"Remove that bitch before I kick it." I was dead serious.

He slipped back inside and picked back up the rhythm.

Wet sloppy sounds and moans filled the room as we made love.

"Imma about to cum!" I yelled out.

His pace increased. "Cum then." He had my hips in a death grip.

"Aaaaawwwww," I moaned, creaming all over him.

Me cumming must have sent him over the edge. He leaned down and bit the back of my neck. Without letting go, he pounded into me. I felt myself building up to another orgasm. Around a mouthful of my skin, he groaned, emptying his seed inside.

He turned us over. I laid down on his chest, closing my eyes.

"Let's shower before you get too tired," he said.

I got up and followed him into our bathroom. He ran the water and I sat on the toilet. Keyz beat my pussy up so well and good, wiping myself stung.

We hopped in the shower and rinsed off without getting frisky. I slipped on my maternity two-piece pajama set before getting back in bed. I laid my head back on Keyz' chest then turned to my side to get into a more comfortable position. I hardly got a good night's sleep since my belly was so big and it was hard for me to get comfortable. Keyz turned over and spooned my body into his. He alternated between rubbing my head and rubbing my stomach. My baby kicked every time he ran his hand on my belly. Between his gentle caresses and the heat emanating from his body, my eyelids got heavy. I was knocked out sleep before I knew it.

I dreamed of holding my precious bundle in my arms. My little baby looked up at me with beautiful chocolate eyes like Keyz. My baby yawned and then smiled, revealing dimples that were identical to mine. A persistent shake disrupted the dream that I was having while peacefully sleeping. Batting away the hand on my shoulder, I attempted to fall back into a deep slumber.

"Wake up, Shaunie," he said, shaking me gently.

Opening my eyes, I looked at him standing over me on the side of the bed. "What?" I asked with an attitude. This was the first time in weeks that I slept that good and I was pissed to have it interrupted. I needed all the sleep I could get, because once the baby arrived, I would sleep on the his clock.

He pulled the covers from off me. "Yo ass done pissed in the bed. Again."

I sat up and sure enough I was laying in a small patch of wetness. "Well, I can't help it. The baby pushes on my bladder." I climbed out the bed.

Keyz began to remove the soiled sheets from the mattress. "We gon' need another mattress fucking with yo ole pissy ass. Shit, Keira don't even piss in the bed," he teased me.

"Shut up." I pushed him as I walked pass him to get to the bathroom.

Once inside the bathroom, I took off my clothes and hopped in the shower to rinse the smell of urine off. While lathering myself, I got the strong urge to pee. I started hopping on my feet to try and keep it in until I was done with my shower.

Quickly getting out the shower, I sat on the toilet to relieve myself. I wiped myself and was about to flush it when something told me to look at the tissue. On the tissue was red and yellow mucus. Immediately, I knew I had just lost my mucus plug. Not thinking anything of it because when I was pregnant with Keira, I lost my mucus plug two weeks before I went into labor, I got dressed in another set of pajamas.

I went back into the room to inform Keyz what happened when I used the bathroom. I took three steps before I felt wetness leaking down my legs. "Keyz!! My water just broke."

He turned to find me standing in a small puddle. "Oh shit. What I need to do? We need to get an ambulance."

I closed my eyes for patience. Normally, I would be nervous about things, but I tried to remind myself that I prepared for this. "You need to get me to the hospital. Grab the bag that I packed. It's in the closet. Go and wake your mom and tell her where we are going. Imma put on some dry clothes."

Keyz practically ran out the room. He could face niggas with guns blazing, but me going into labor sends him in a panic. I chuckled to myself. He was the same way when we had Keira. While he did what I told him, I changed clothes and grabbed the bag out the closet, since I knew he was going to forget.

"Come on, let's go," he said when he came back into the room.

"Where are you going dressed like that?" I asked. He had on the official fuck gear. Fuck gear was the clothes most hood niggas wore when they went over to a girl's house to lay dick down. He had on sweat pants, without boxers, because I saw his dick swinging. A wife beater did nothing to hide his burly chest. On his feet were white socks and some Nike slippers.

"Man, fuck all that. We need to get going."

I smacked my teeth at him. Then I was shocked at myself, because I rarely did that. Nikki had me picking up her bad habits. "At least put some drawers on. I don't want no bitches bird watching when your dick swinging everywhere."

He clenched his jaw then stormed to the dresser and pulled out some boxers. Slipping them on without a word, he turned back to me. Bending slightly, he picked me up and carried me to the car. He pulled off burning rubber. We hopped on the interstate and headed to Touro Hospital as we drove in silence with the music playing in the background. I sent a text to my mom and Nikki. I rubbed my stomach to help sooth my nerves. Thoughts of my baby and who would be revealed as the father raced through my head. Keyz promised to be there with us no matter the outcome, but I was still worried.

Getting off on the exit, he made a sharp right turn. In doing so, he hit one of the many potholes that the city of New Orleans took their sweet time to repair. Hitting the bump caused a sharp pain to shoot through my stomach. I bent over holding my stomach as I turned to breathe. The pain took the air out of me.

"Watch the fucking bumps!" I screamed. Childbirth would bring out the worst in a woman.

"My bad, bae."

I looked over at him with evil eyes. My hand itched to slap the shit out of him with that my bad shit. My stomach clenched and tightened. My first contraction hit me just as soon as we turned on the street of the hospital.

Keyz parked the car in the parking garage. Hopping out the car, he came over to my side and helped me out the car. I tried to walk, but he lifted me and the bag in his arms and walked quickly inside the emergency room doors.

No sooner had we walked inside, another contraction hit. "Uuurrgghh." I panted, clutching my belly. The contractions were coming four minutes apart.

"My wife is in labor. We need the doctor."

A nurse came from around the triage station. She grabbed a wheelchair and Keyz placed me in it.

The nurse wheeled me to labor and delivery. The whole while she asked me questions about my due date, doctor's name, pain level, and how far apart I estimated my contractions. I tried my best to answer her, but the contractions were hitting closer. Keyz walked beside me and answered when I couldn't.

A labor and delivery nurse met us at the elevator. She took over my care after the other nurse shared the information I had given her. I was placed inside a room and they helped me on the bed after I changed into a hospital gown. The nurse hooked me up to a Doppler and then made me lean back with my feet in the foot rests to check my cervix.

She informed me that I was in active labor and that she was going to call my doctor. I told her I wanted an epidural before I progressed too far for it. She nodded then left.

Keyz came to my side, stroking my head. "You ready?"

Honestly, I was afraid to finally have an answer for the question I asked myself the entire pregnancy.

"Yes." Another contraction hit. Keyz reminded me to breathe through it. I nodded, exhaled and inhaled. The pain was excruciating. When it subsided enough for me to think straight, I asked him, "What if it isn't your baby?" I just needed to ask again. I never imagined myself having several baby daddies. In most urban areas, it was common for women to have multiple baby daddies. However, I didn't want to be another statistic. Besides, I was raised with conservative values. No babies out of wedlock and certainly not multiple children out of wedlock. My situation certainly didn't fit the mold of the values I was taught. Key couldn't understand why I wanted him to be the father of my unborn. Besides being the man I loved, I didn't want my kids to have different fathers and different last names.

"I ain't gon' lie and say I'm not gon' be fucked up about it, because it's gon' hurt a nigga. You the one who wants the DNA test, not me. Imma be here regardless. At the end of the day the baby still mine. Hell, he might come out looking like me, either way, since I been feeding him."

I laughed at his silly statement. The easy banter between us helped me to relax some. Keyz sat on the sofa texting on his phone. No doubt telling the crew I was in labor. I worked through the contraction. The anesthesiologist came in my room and administered the epidural.

Soon after, the doctor came. Dr. Buras checked my cervix and told me I had dilated fully and it was time to push. The nurses came in and made sure everything was ready for the delivery. My doctor rolled his chair to the foot of my bed and lifted up the sheet. Keyz came over and helped me hold my legs up so I could push.

"On the count of three," the doctor said.

I nodded and waited for the count of three before I gave a big push. My face felt hot from the strain of pushing. The doctor told me to stop pushing when the contraction ended. I fell back on the bed to rest. Not a second later, a contraction hit and I had the urge to push.

"Breathe, bae, breathe."

"I am fucking breathing!" I screamed at Keyz like a raving lunatic. Why do people tell a delivering woman the dumbest shit? I pushed hard and felt something breaching my vagina.

"The head is crowning. A few more big pushes should do it," the doctor told me.

At the moment, I didn't think I had it in me. I was exhausted and tired. I just wanted to give up. My hormones were raging out of control. Between crying, feeling joy, or screaming, I didn't know what emotion or reaction to choose from.

I looked up at Keyz with glistening eyes. "You are going to leave me," I started sobbing, referring to what I thought he was going to do when the baby came. The nurse and doctor didn't pay us any mind. They must surely be used to dealing with an overwrought female.

Keyz squeezed my hand, hard. "Stop talking stupid. Ain't nobody going nowhere. Now let's push this baby out. Keira and Shaun ready to meet their baby brother."

Another contraction came and I pushed with all my might. Two more pushes and I brought forth life. Tears of joy ran freely from my eyes when a loud wail filled the room. Keyz had a proud smirk on his face.

"It's a baby boy," the doctor announced, holding my baby up. I couldn't wait to hold him in my arms. "Dad, do you want to cut the cord?"

"Fa sho.'" Keyz walked to the foot of the bed and cut the cord. The nurse quickly wrapped him before placing my baby in my arms.

I looked down at my sweet baby. He didn't look like anyone, he looked like all babies did when first born. "I love you," I whispered to him as I lifted him up to get his scent.

The nurse came over to take him to be cleaned and weighed. Another nurse cleaned me up down there as best as she could get until I was able to shower. They took my baby away to do his newborn check-up and I was missing him already.

Keyz sat on the bed next to me. "You did good, ma." He leaned down and kissed my sweaty forehead.

"I love you."

"I love you too. So, what name are we going with?"

We had gone back and forth on names. Finally, we agreed on one we both liked. "Kelan Stacy."

"Kelan Stacy." He paused. "You mean Kelan Stacy Jones."

I looked at him and smiled. We agreed that no matter what, the baby would carry Keyz' last name. I didn't fight it. Even if the baby wasn't his, my child's biological father wasn't alive anyway. "Yes, bae. Kelan Stacy Jones."

The events of the night exhausted me. But I fell to sleep with a smile on my face. I had the love of my life in my life and I just gave birth to a beautiful, healthy baby boy.

Chapter 29

A man that shows consistency will never have to worry about her loyalty.

-*Unknown*

Keyz

I sat on the sofa holding Kelan. He looked all pudgy and red with a head full of hair that stood up all over his head. Looking over at the bed, Shaunie was sleeping peacefully. My girl was tired from the ordeal of pushing an eight pound, twenty-one inch baby out. We had visitors for the past few hours. My brother, Kamal, and his girl, came down to see the baby and dropped off a gift. Nikki came down shortly after Kelan was delivered. She snapped a bunch of pictures of my lil' man and posted them on Instagram and Facebook. She hogged the baby and no one got a chance to hold him while she was here.

Rayne and Thugga came together, bringing us food from Houston's Restaurant to celebrate the birth of my second son. We all sat around and talked about what was happening in the hood. The nurse came to assist Shaunie at feeding time for the baby. She whipped out her tits like it was a bottle and started feeding Kelan. My boys sat there in shock, mouths and eyes wide open, before leaving the room. Nikki and Shaunie burst out laughing at them niggas.

Shaunie's mom came down and shut all the shenanigans down. She was old school when it came to childbirth. Her motto was it was bonding time for mom, dad, and baby. My peeps visited ten more minutes then she informed everybody that her daughter needed her rest, especially since my mom had yet to bring Keira and Shaun to meet Kelan.

The room was full of flowers, balloons, and gifts. Our room was the liveliest on the entire floor. Hell, probably the whole hospital.

The TV was on, but I was too engrossed in watching my girl and baby. Just like his mama, he slept with is bottle lip poking out. I saw nothing but Shaunie when I looked at him.

Noticing he was sleeping, I stood up and walked to the bassinet that was beside the bed. Gently, I laid him down then walked back to the sofa where I was sitting. Getting comfortable, I laid back in the chair. Just when I closed my eyes, the door creaked open. I was expecting my mama and the kids, but it was a nurse. In her hand was a brown envelope that I was thinking was the DNA testing results.

"Good morning, Mr. Jones. I have the results for the paternity test," she said, confirming what I already knew.

I stood up and accepted the envelope. "Thank you." Waiting until she was out the room, I looked over at Shaunie before tearing open the envelope and removing the sheet of paper. My hands trembled a bit as I unfolded the paper and began reading the results.

In the case of Kelan Stacy Jones, the alleged father, Keyon Jones, is excluded as the biological father. The Combined Paternity Index (CPI) is 0 and the Probability of Paternity is 0%.

I looked over at the bed and shook my head. Shaunie was going to be crushed at the results. She had hoped it was mine. Damn. I couldn't even lie and say I wasn't fucked up about it either. Against all hope, I had hoped he was mine, too. I didn't want him growing up not knowing who he was or who his family was. Kelan being mine would have made everything easier. My hopes were purely unselfish. I came to accept the fact that Shaunie had been with another nigga, so that wasn't the issue. I grew up without my father, so I wanted the best for him and having his father was the best. I may not be the biological father, but I would be a father were it counted. Quickly coming to a decision, I grabbed the envelope and stood up. I left the room and headed to the lab downstairs. Being that the beige nigga was dead there was no point in even upsetting Shaunie or making her feel bad that the baby wasn't mine. My lil' nigga was gon' grow up and be raised a Jones.

I crept back in the room and placed a sealed envelope on the nightstand next to Shaunie's bed. It took a minute to convince the technician to do what I wanted. He looked at me in disbelief that I wanted the results to confirm me as the father. Most niggas would try to bribe him to exclude them. In the end, money talked and I had plenty of it to do what needed to be done for my family.

Noise from the bed alerted me that Shaunie was moving around and waking up. I leaned back in the chair and pretended to have dosed off.

"Keyz," she whispered, but I didn't answer.

I was glad my head was turned away from her because a smile threatened to erupt. Wanting my fake sleep to be more believable, I let out a snore.

She smacked her teeth. A pillow hit my face. I jerked at the contact to seem like I was jolted awake.

"Man, what?" I asked in a husky, sleepy voice.

"I need to use the bathroom. Can you help me?"

I stood up, pulled my pants up then walked over to the bed. Standing on her side as she leaned on me for support, she used the bathroom and I helped her back to the bed. I made sure she was on the side closest to the nightstand so the brown envelope could catch her attention.

We were almost to the bed when she noticed it. "Keyz, what's in the envelope?"

I shrugged my shoulder, playing it off. "I dunno know. I was knocked out. One of the nurses must have set it there while we were sleeping."

Her hand clenched mine. "I think it's the results," she said in a small voice that hitched.

"Maybe, let's get you back in bed." I helped her climb back in the bed and get settled before I turned to go back to the sofa.

"Can you hand it to me?" she asked.

I had to keep myself from smiling. A nigga was playing it off like an actor. Hell, I deserved an Oscar for the performance I was putting on. I picked the envelope up and gave it to her, nonchalantly.

She grabbed it and held it for several heartbeats. She seemed unsure or afraid to read it. With a huge sigh, she opened the envelope and read the altered results.

"Oh my god." Her hands covered her mouth and she looked up at me. "Bae, Kelan is yours." She started kicking her legs in excitement and relief. "He's yours."

I walked over to the bed and yanked the results from her hand. Reading over it quickly, I smiled at how happy she was that he was mine. The unknown had been weighing heavily on her, on top of dealing with the death of her friend and mine. I was just glad I was able to bring a little sliver of joy to our situation.

"I'm glad, bae. But you do know it didn't matter. He would have been anyway."

"I know. I just needed to know. It was eating me alive not knowing."

A tiny pang of guilt shot through me at the thought of deceiving her, but what was done now couldn't be undone. Plus, the results wouldn't change how I felt about the baby. I just hoped she never found out about me having the results altered.

"It's over now." I kissed her lips. I couldn't resist when she looked up at me with all her love for me reflected in her eyes.

We started to get into the kiss, but a wail interrupted us. Breaking apart, we laughed. That would be our life and intimate moments for the next few years.

I picked Kelan up and cradled him in my arms as I carried him to his mama. Shaunie took him from me.

"Mommy's lil' man is hungry." Kelan was gnawing on his hand. She slipped her robe down and positioned him to her breast. Immediately, he began to root around for her nipple. She placed it to his lips and he latched on. I watched as he suckled nourishment from her.

I never gave thought to a woman breastfeeding her baby. But watching my woman giving our baby nourishment was the most beautiful act known to mankind, in my eyes. Seeing her being so nurturing made me fall in love with her more, if that was even possible. I was transfixed watching them. She switched breasts and Kelan latched on without a problem. His little jaws worked as he pulled milk.

Shaunie looked up at me and smiled. "What?"

"Nothing. Just watching my son."

Her smile was radiant at the reminder that Kelan was mine. The relief could be seen in her eyes. I didn't understand why she was so worried over whether the baby was mine or not when the outcome wouldn't have changed anything. She tried to explain about how she didn't want to fit with the stereotype of black women having several baby daddies. The way I feel about it was fuck it. Nobody had to take care of shit this way, so let people classify the situation how they wanted. I watched as she continued to nurse the baby. When she was done, I offered to burp him. I walked around the room as I gently patted his back. After he burped, I laid him in the bassinet and changed his diaper like a pro. This wasn't my first rodeo with a baby. I often changed Keira when she was a baby. I was a hands-on daddy.

Kelan lay quietly in his bassinet. Shaunie and I watched some TV for a while. The nurse came to check on Shaunie and the baby. After weighing Kelan's soiled diapers and checking Shaunie, she left with a promise to return in a few hours.

Not long after, Shaunie dozed off. I pulled my phone from out my sweatpants pocket to call my mom to see what was taking her so long to bring the kids up to the hospital to meet their brother.

Me: Hey ma. Where y'all at?

In less than a minute I got a response back.

Mama: Don't be rushing me! We coming up on the elevator now.

I quietly walked out the room to meet them at the elevator. The bell dinged and the doors slid open. My daughter's face lit up when she saw me. Shaun hadn't noticed me. He pulled her back when she tried to take off running to me. I needed to have a talk with him and tell him good looking out for taking care of his sister like a big brother should.

"Daddy! Daddy!" Keira screamed as she shook Shaun off and ran to me.

My mom and Shaun looked up at my approach.

Opening my arms and bending slightly, I picked my baby girl up and engulfed her in my arms. Every day I made sure to let her know how much I loved her. I never wanted my baby girl to grow up feeling insecure or inadequate because she has daddy issues. A nigga was going to have to be about his business and treat my daughter like a queen to retain her attention. I made many mistakes in my life and some of the things I did with her mama, but I always made sure to show Keira attention and love. I'd be damned if she'd be like some of these chicks out here looking for love in all the wrong places.

"Hey daddy's baby girl." I kissed her cheek. She wrapped her little arms around my neck. "Are you ready to meet your baby brother?"

"No!" She folded her arms across her chest and pouted. She was excited at the thought of a new baby. But I guess when faced with reality, she changed her mind.

My mama laughed at her. "Child, y'all gon' have y'alls hands full with her spoiled behind."

Keira was spoiled and I wanted her that way.

"Don't be like that. You have to be a good big sister just like Shaun is a good big brother, okay?" My son was a good kid and a

214

good big brother. He looked out for his sister. He played with her and helped her when she needed him.

She looked thoughtful before she reluctantly replied. "Okay, daddy."

I looked down at Shaun. He was starting to look more and more like me. "What's up, my big man?" I crouched down until I was his level and opened my arms so he could come over and give me a hug.

"Hey daddy." He hug me. I patted his head once I stood up I looked down at him with a smile on my face. My heart filled with so much love and pride. Despite everything he had been through, he never once misbehaved or acted out. I was blessed not to have a hell-raiser like I was.

He stepped back. I looked at my mama. She stood with a smile on her face, watching as I had a moment with my kids.

"Hey, ma." I leaned over and kissed her cheek.

"Come on, Keyz. I'm ready to go and see my new grandson."

We turned and headed to the room. Shaunie and Kelan was still sleep. My mom went to the sink and washed her and the kids' hands. When they were done, I picked Keira up and held her over the bassinet so she could see the baby. Shaun stood on his tip-toes and peeked over the edge.

Sensing people in the room, Shaunie woke up from her nap. Keira shrieked to be held by her mom. I sat her on the bed and she crawled over to her lap.

"Mommy, I missed you." She jumped around in Shaunie's lap. Shaunie winced at the contact.

"Be careful, Keira, so you don't hurt mommy," I reminded her.

She kissed her daughter's cheek and hugged her back. "I missed you too."

Shaunie looked up and her eyes sought something behind me. She quickly looked at me then looked behind me again. I turned and saw Shaun standing in the back. He looked a little sad, but I didn't know the reason why.

Now that I think on it, he had been a little withdrawal the past few days and he hardly said anything since he arrived. He was usually very talkative. I stepped back and pulled him to my side.

"Hey Shaun," Shaunie said with a bright smile.

He scuffled his foot while looking at the floor. "Hey."

Shaunie and I shared a look.

"Did you see the baby?" Shaunie asked him. He nodded. "Isn't he cute?"

He shrugged his shoulder. "I guess."

"What's the matter, son?" I intervened, wanting to know what was weighing on my son's mind.

He looked up at me then looked to Shaunie before putting his head down. His eyes glistened with unshed tears. Getting worried that something might have happened to him, I called his name to get his attention.

His little voice broke when he spoke. "Y'all gon' send me away now that y'all have another son."

My mama and Shaunie gasped. Keira, unaware of the situation kept playing in her mama's hair. I felt like shit hearing what was wrong with my son. Not once did I take into consideration how the new addition would make him feel. He seemed to just fit with the family, so I never thought he would be insecure about his place with us. My heart broke looking at his bottom lip tremble. He was trying to be a big boy and not cry.

I kneeled down and took his head in my hand, forcing him to look at me. "Shaun, ain't nobody sending you away. You are a part of this family. It doesn't matter if we have ten more boys, you are here to stay. You will just be the big brother to them all. I don't ever want you to feel like you don't belong with us. We love you."

"But Shaunie isn't my mama. I don't have a mama anymore."

My mom turned away with an angry expression on her face. I knew she turned away to keep from saying something negative about Ashley in front of Shaun. She walked over to the crib and picked Kelan up. I was having a hard time schooling my features so I didn't further upset Shaun. I didn't want him to think I was mad at him. On the inside though, I was boiling with anger.

I wanted to strangle that bitch, Ashley, for the pain she caused my son. I don't know what went wrong with the situation. Before Shaunie found out about Shaun, Ashley was a decent mother to him. After Shaunie found out, Ashley seemed to change overnight, slowly but surely. She went from taking care of my child to neglecting and beating him. She hadn't been around since I found the bruises all over Shaun's body and her ass was arrested. It would do her well to stay the fuck out of dodge. If I ever caught up with her ass, she was dead. Baby mama or not.

Keira picked a fine time to chime in. "You can call my mama, mama." She looked at him with an expression that said "duh" like it was just that simple. I almost laughed at how smart and observant she was.

He looked up at Shaunie as if to gauge her reaction at the suggestion.

Shaunie beckoned him over to her. He slowly walked over to the bed. She placed her hand on his cheek.

"I know I can never replace your mom. But I love you just like you are my son. I don't mind if you call me mom. I would love nothing more. You have a mom. Right here. Me. I'm your mother now." She looked up at me, waiting to see if I would object. "That's if your daddy says it's okay."

This is why I loved this woman. She was so unselfish. Getting past her hurt and pain, she accepted my child as her own. In that moment, I was glad I made the decision to alter the DNA results. We were a family no matter whose loins the seeds sprouted from.

Shaun turned to me with a hopeful expression on his face. I nodded my head in approval. "You can call her mom, son."

He turned back to her. "Okay mama."

Shaunie held out her arms for him. I picked him up and sat him on the bed next to her. She pulled him in her arms and wrapped him in her embrace. "I love you so much. I don't want you to ever feel like you don't belong to me. I'm so glad you are a part of our family." She leaned down and kissed his cheek.

We all breathed a sigh of relief that everything went well.

"Alright everybody. Y'all gather next to the bed," my mama said. She gave me my son and I cradled him in my arms. "I want to get some pictures of the happy little family."

Keira sat in her mama's lap, Shaun stood next to me on the side of the bed, and I held Kelan while my mama snapped pictures.

We passed Kelan around so everyone could hold him, all the while capturing those moments with pictures.

Chapter 30

Pride attracts the girl. Courage approaches the girl. Wisdom gets the girl. Strength puts up with the girl, but loyalty keeps the girl.

-Unknown

Shaunie

I stood in the back pacing the floor, the train of my dress trailing behind me and my heels clicking on the floor. I was anxious to begin the start of our journey as husband and wife. Today was just the start of a lifetime of love and life. It took us seven years to get here. Seven years of many storms, some with tragic outcomes. As passionately as I loved Keyz, I got tired of the drama and pain. Keyz refused to let me go and pursued be relentlessly. Waiting for the music to start, I couldn't keep myself from wearing a hole in the floor. Sitting down or standing still was impossible with all this excess energy flowing through me. My energy wasn't from nervousness or uncertainty, but from anxiously wanting to begin this chapter of my life. Finally, today was my wedding day and I couldn't have asked for a more perfect day.

The weather was amazing. The sun shone and it was right at eighty-four degrees. The fall foliage was a perfect backdrop. Our wedding and reception was being held at Popp Fountain and Arbor Room at Popp Fountain in New Orleans City Park.

The only thing missing was my father, Stacy and Killer. It's still so hard to believe that we were getting married and both of our best friends weren't here to witness this moment, long awaited as it was.

The music started playing. Uncle Mike turned to me. "Are you ready, Shaunie?" he asked with a smile. He was walking me down the aisle since my father wasn't alive to do so.

"Yes." I turned toward the door, grabbed his arm that he offered and waited for the music to change.

"You look beautiful."

I turned to him and smiled. Uncle Mike was one of the realest people I knew. I was so glad he was walking me down the aisle in place of my father. "Thank you, Uncle Mike. I'm so glad you were able to walk me today."

He patted my hand. "It's a privilege. Since day one I considered you part of the family. I'm glad we are finally making it official."

The music played as the wedding party walked ahead of me. I didn't have a big bridal party. My bridesmaids were Nikki and Minnie. Keira was the flower girl and Shaun was the ring bearer.

Keira was excited to walk down the aisle in her dress that was a replica of mine. I heard people snickering, so I was imagining which of my kids did something that had the wedding guests laughing. At rehearsal, my daughter pranced down the aisle dropping the flower petals. Then she would stop and start to play with them. It was hard remembering that she was only three-years-old, because sometimes she acted much older in some of the things she did. But other times she would do things that any other three-year-old did.

It was hard getting Shaun excited to wear a suit. Keyz told me during the fitting for his tux, he complained the entire time. He pouted for rehearsal and stated that he didn't see the point in walking down the aisle holding a pillow with rings on it.

The traditional bridal music started. Immediately, I got focused. Uncle Mike and I began a slow pace to the front where Keyz and the minister waited. When we stepped on the cream carpet that had been rolled out, the guests stood.

I saw that my bridesmaids, the groomsmen, Keira, and Shaun had taken their place at the front like it was practiced. My dress trailed behind me as I walked gracefully down the aisle. I took slow measured steps to ensure I didn't fall on my face for my special day. Clutching Uncle Mike's arm, I held on a little tighter at the thought of falling.

My eyes connected with Keyz from afar. In my mind's eyes, I saw our life together before this moment. Our journey together played like a movie in my mind. The day I met Keyz was as clear today as it was the very first day.

"What's up, shorty. You need a ride?" he licked his lips and gave me a cocky smile.

I looked up with a "what you think" face.

"I don't get in cars with strangers, but thank you." My eyes were averted from him.

He smiled at me. "I feel ya. Give me yo number so I don't be a stranger for long."

"I'll pass," I replied with a deadpan expression on my face and looked right back down to my book.

Keyz supporting me through school and giving me encouragement:

Enveloping me in a tight hug, Keyz said, "I'm so proud of you, bae."

"I couldn't have done it without you, baby. I love you."

"No, bae. You did it by yourself. You paid for school and got the grades. I wasn't there in the class with you. The credit is all yours."

Keyz pursuing me when I gave up on us.

"I told you it's over, Keyon. See yourself out."

"We ain't never gon' be over. The only thing that could ever end us is death," he said, causing my heart to skip a beat and shivers down my spine.

Keyz telling me how I made him a better man:

His thumb moved back and forth, caressing my cheek. "But you, you make me feel like a man. With you, I am a man. You let me be the provider and protector of you and our child. You allowed me to do things for you, even when you don't really need me."

I shook my head at the memories before I focused back on the love of my life. He had an enormous smile on his face. I beamed back at him. When our eyes connected, it felt like it was just us, even though we were surrounded by people. There was no nervousness from us. We both knew we wanted to be with each other, so the dramatics and hysterics weren't needed.

The venue was packed with family and friends who came to show their support as Keyz and I were joined together as man and wife. Flashes could be seen all around as people snapped picture after picture to capture this moment. I knew it wasn't going to be long before several of the pictures were going to circulate on Facebook and Instagram. I was fine with that.

I got closer to the front. My mom, who held Kelan on her lap, sat next to Ms. Lynn. Both of them were smiling from ear to ear. My baby was sitting up trying to eat his fingers. He was the chubbiest four month old baby I ever saw. I gave them a small smile when I passed them.

Stopping, we took our place next to Keyz. Uncle Mike gave me away and I took my rightful place next to my soon-to-be husband. The minster gave a speech then proceeded to read a verse from the bible about man and woman joining as one. He turned to us and told us it was time to say our vows. We decided to write our own simple vows. I don't know how long it took Keyz to write his, but I took a full week to write mine. The perfect words came to me in parts. Some nights while sleeping, I would dream of saying my vows. I would wake up remembering some of the words and write them down. Other times the words came to me while listening to music or just going about different daily chores.

We turned to face each other, looking the other in the eyes. Looking in the eyes of the man I loved, I saw my past, present, and my future. "You are my one and only love. I'm blessed to have a beautiful, smart, generous, and caring woman at my side. To help make a home for us. You held me down and helped me to stand when I stumbled. You inspire me to be a better man. As I stand by your side today, I vow to cherish and honor you, remain faithful to you, and love you until the end of time. And our next lifetime." My eyes watered and tears threatened to fall as I stood there listening to him vow his life to me. His words were so heartfelt. Seeing that I was at the point of crying, Keyz gave my hands a gentle squeeze before completing his vows. "At your side is where I belong and shall remain through the pressures of the present and the uncertainties of our future. All that I have, all that I am, all that I will ever be, is yours."

His words resonated in me. What he said was exactly how I felt. In spite of everything we had been through, we were still together and standing stronger than ever. We are stronger because our love had been tested several times, but our destiny was together.

Not missing a beat of looking away from his eyes, I began my vows. "I take you, Keyon Jones, as my partner for life. I gave you my hand and my heart so that we may walk hand in hand through whatever life may throw our way or wherever our journey takes us." I paused to swallow the lump in my throat. Tears tracked down my cheeks. Keyz gently wiped them away with the pad of his thumb. His eyes looked moist as if tears were pending. "I promise to be your friend, your lover, and your ally, in good and bad times, sorrow and success, sickness and health. Now, forever, eternity."

Shaun stepped up to the wedding official and held up the pillow with the rings. He blessed the rings by praying over them. When he was done, Shaun turned to us so we could place the rings of each other's hand.

Not long after, we were pronounced man and wife. Our guests applauded and some stood up when we were done. After seven years and three kids, I was finally Mrs. Keyon Jones.

Epilogue

The secret of a good life is to have the right loyalties and hold them in the right scale of value.

-*Norman Matton Thomas*

Keyz

The sound of tinkling laughter could be heard through the house. I quietly slipped in the front door and headed to the living room where the sounds were coming from. Shaunie and the kids were so engrossed in the movie they were watching that they hadn't noticed me walk in.

Leaning against the wall, I took in the sight of my family. My baby girl was going on five and will be starting school soon. She was the spitting image of her mama, inside and out. She was going to be a gorgeous woman when she grew up. But the main quality she possessed was how nurturing and caring she was. Even at this age I could see that she was going to have a gentle soul with quiet strength, especially in how she took care of her brothers.

I knew many people thought that Shaunie was stupid and weak for dealing with me and everything that I put her through. What people failed to realize was she wasn't stupid and was far from weak. Any woman can throw in the towel and call a wrap when times get hard. That was easy. Being able to deal with your problems head on and to go for what you want without listening to what people said was hard. Many times we let what people say influence our actions and decisions when they aren't the ones who had to live with those decisions.

Finally taking notice of me, she turned my way. Her eyes lit up as she stood. I pushed off the wall and met her halfway. "Hey bae." She stepped into my arms and I held her before leaning down and kissing her lips.

"I missed you," I said against her lips. I had been gone four days taking care of some business in Miami with my connect.

"I missed you too."

"Daddy!" Keira ran to me, almost knocking her mama out the way to get my attention. She wrapped her arms around my legs. Shaun picked up Kelan and walked over to us.

"Hey dad."

"What's up, my big boy?" I pulled him closer to me and hugged him. Shaun was an amazing big brother. He helped around the house and looked after his siblings. He was happier now that he had a mother in Shaunie. Ashley still hadn't appeared and I was cool with that. Shaun stopped asking for and about her many months ago. His life was full with us. He just started playing football on the same team as Lil' Thugga and he did competitive swimming for his school.

"I'm good. Keke has been asking for you every day. And Kel been giving mama the blues with all that crying." I already knew Keira was a daddy's girl, so it was no surprise that she whined for me. Kelan was spoiled. My lil'man like for me to hold him and play with him. When Shaunie went in to the daycare centers to check in on the staff, me and him hung out. I didn't want my son to go to daycare so early, so I kept him home with me.

I took Kelan from his arms then turned and looked at Shaunie. I cocked my eyebrows at her and she was struggling to contain her laughter as Shaun gave his report of what happened in my absence.

"Alright, my babies. It's time for bed," she told the kids.

The kids groaned, but turned toward the staircase to go to their rooms. Shaunie and I followed behind them. We put the kids to bed then went to our room. I stripped out my clothes, leaving my boxers on and climbed under the sheets.

"So, how did it go?" Shaunie asked about the Miami trip.

"It's done. I'm out the game and Thugga taking over. Alejandro said he knew the day was coming for me to leave the game." After

226

getting married, my whole mindset changed. My priorities were crystal clear. The game helped me to build what I have today, but I couldn't let it tear apart my family. I had been extremely lucky in that I hadn't been arrested or killed during my reign of the streets.

She kissed her name that was tatted on my chest, over my heart. "Well, I'm glad. We have enough money invested and several lucrative businesses. I'll rather be poor than lose you to the streets or jail."

"Baby, I ain't going nowhere. Everything I need is right here."

"I love you."

"I love you too." I meant every word I said. Life couldn't be better. I had my family and my health. What more could a man ask for?

Shaunie

Life was great. I had my kids and my husband. It wasn't easy to get to this point in our life, but we did. Sometimes we have to weather a storm to get to where we are meant to be. Anyone can love you when the sun is shining, but in the storms is where you learn who truly loves you and holds your best interest at heart.

I looked over to Keyz who slept on his side of the bed. This man had brought me so much joy and so much pain in the years we have been together. But the joy outweighed everything else. It's easy for us to remember all the bad things. However, never lose sight of the good.

I have been called many things. From stupid, to weak, to being a gold digger. None of the things people said about me mattered. At the end of the day, this was my life and I was going to live it how I wanted.

With a smile, I placed my hand on my belly and rubbed in a circular motion. Not being able to contain my surprise any longer, I slid closer to my husband.

"Keyz." I shook him to wake him up. He went to sleep before I could tell him my news.

"Huh," he mumbled.

"Wake up. It's important," I said urgently.

He popped up and grabbed his heater from the nightstand, ever prepared to defend us with his life.

I chuckled at how fast he was up when he thought there was trouble. "Baby, nothing is wrong."

"What's up, ma?"

Smiling, I grabbed his hand and placed it on my stomach. His eyes widened before he threw me a cocky grin. "So, a nigga done knocked you up again?"

I nodded my head then straddled him. "And you know how horny I get." I raised my gown over my head and tossed it to the floor.

"Yeah." He licked his lips.

"Yeah." I leaned down and took his mouth in a passionate kiss that had my toes curling. We celebrated the new life we created by making love the rest of the night. There will be many more challenges to come I was sure, but just like we got through them before, we will get through them again. Together, forever, and for all eternity.

The End.

Coming Soon From Lock Down Publications

RESTRAINING ORDER

By **CA$H & COFFEE**

GANGSTA CITY **II**

By **Teddy Duke**

BLOOD OF A BOSS **III**

By **Askari**

THE KING CARTEL **III**

By **Frank Gresham**

SHE DON'T DESERVE THE DICK

SILVER PLATTER HOE **III**

By **Reds Johnson**

BROOKLYN ON LOCK **III**

By **Sonovia Alexander**

THE STREETS BLEED MURDER **III**

By **Jerry Jackson**

CONFESSIONS OF A DOPEMAN'S DAUGHTER **III**

By **Rasstrina**

NEVER LOVE AGAIN **II**

WHAT ABOUT US **II**

By **Kim Kaye**

A DANGEROUS LOVE **VII**

By **J Peach**

A GANGSTER'S REVENGE **II**

By **Aryanna**

GIVE ME THE REASON

Nikki Tee

By **Coco Amoure**

Available Now

LOVE KNOWS NO BOUNDARIES **I II & III**

By **Coffee**

SILVER PLATTER HOE **I & II**

HONEY DIPP **I & II**

CLOSED LEGS DON'T GET FED **I & II**

A BITCH NAMED KARMA

By **Reds Johnson**

A DANGEROUS LOVE **I, II, III, IV, V, VI**

By **J Peach**

CUM FOR ME

An **LDP Erotica Collaboration**

A GANGSTER'S REVENGE

By **Aryanna**

WHAT ABOUT US

NEVER LOVE AGAIN

By **Kim Kaye**

THE KING CARTEL **I & II**

By **Frank Gresham**

BLOOD OF A BOSS **I & II**

By **Askari**

THE DEVIL WEARS TIMBS **I, II & III**

BURY ME A G **I II & III**

By **Tranay Adams**

THESE NIGGAS AIN'T LOYAL **I & II**

By **Nikki Tee**

THE STREETS BLEED MURDER

By **Jerry Jackson**

DIRTY LICKS

By **Peter Mack**

THE ULTIMATE BETRAYAL

By **Phoenix**

BROOKLYN ON LOCK **I & II**

By **Sonovia Alexander**

SLEEPING IN HEAVEN, WAKING IN HELL **I, II & III**

By **Forever Redd**

DON'T FU#K WITH MY HEART **I & II**

By **Linnea**

BOSS'N UP **I & II**

By **Royal Nicole**

LOYALTY IS BLIND

By **Kenneth Chisholm**

<u>BOOKS BY LDP'S CEO, CA$H</u>

TRUST NO MAN

TRUST NO MAN 2

TRUST NO MAN 3

BONDED BY BLOOD

SHORTY GOT A THUG

A DIRTY SOUTH LOVE

THUGS CRY

THUGS CRY 2

TRUST NO BITCH

TRUST NO BITCH 2

TRUST NO BITCH 3

TIL MY CASKET DROPS

Coming Soon

TRUST NO BITCH (KIAM EYEZ' STORY)

THUGS CRY 3

BONDED BY BLOOD 2

RESTRANING ORDER

www.ingramcontent.com/pod-product-compliance
Lightning Source LLC
Chambersburg PA
CBHW071324250626
47159CB00004B/1457